THE LAST STORM

JACK HUNT

DIRECT RESPONSE PUBLISHING

Published by Direct Response Publishing

ISBN-13: 978-1721768837
ISBN-10: 1721768831

Also By Jack Hunt

The Renegades

The Renegades 2: Aftermath

The Renegades 3: Fortress

The Renegades 4: Colony

The Renegades 5: United

Mavericks: Hunters Moon

Killing Time

State of Panic

State of Shock

State of Decay

Defiant

Phobia

Anxiety

Strain

Blackout

Darkest Hour

Final Impact

And Many More…

Dedication

For my family.

Chapter 1

October 9

Whittier, Alaska

Officer Danny Lee banged furiously on the door of apartment 1002. He heard the sound of a shuffle then footsteps approaching. There was a pause as the occupant took a second to peer through the peephole.

"Greg! Open up. Let's go," Danny said before glancing nervously down the pale yellow hallway. Several locks were cleared and the green door cracked opened. Greg Mitchell was in his late twenties. He looked like a rat with a slanted forehead, gaunt cheeks, a goatee, and a long, dark ponytail exposed beneath an orange beanie cap. He always wore the same clothes: raggedy old jeans, scuffed military ankle boots and a black winter jacket with numerous patches sewn into it. A half-smoked cigarette hung from the corner of his mouth, blue smoke spiraling up into his eye causing him to squint. He flashed stained teeth and was about to say something when Danny barged in, shoving him out of the way.

"Where is it?" Danny demanded to know.

His eyes surveyed the cockroach-infested apartment before he darted into the bathroom. The sink had hard-water stains, and there was a shit in the bottom of the toilet. The floor wasn't much better — a mat looked as if he'd spilled some black hair dye on it then tried to scrub it out. Danny winced as he backed out.

"It's safe, hidden away in apartment 1003, just like you asked."

Danny scowled. "Not the heroin, you idiot. The—"

Before he finished Danny got his answer. He entered

the spare bedroom and took in the sight of a full-scale grow op with high-powered lights, a ventilation system and hydroponic equipment designed to handle about twenty marijuana plants in full bloom. Of course he knew Greg had a couple but not this many. He staggered back a few steps, gripping his head.

"You have got to be kidding me."

Greg shrugged. "What? It's all legal and aboveboard."

He stared on, dumbfounded by his stupidity. "Legal?" Danny spat back. He whirled around and grabbed a fistful of his shirt. "It might be legal, idiot, but there are restrictions, such as cultivating only six plants with no more than three in the mature stage. You are looking at more than one ounce here, Greg."

"And?"

"That's a C felony in Alaska. Or for someone dumb like you, it means spending up to five years behind bars and a fine up to fifty thousand dollars."

Greg's mouth opened but nothing came out. Danny thrust him away and turned back to the room. His thoughts were racing. “You need to get this shit out of here now.”

“What? We’re trafficking heroin and you’re worried about a few marijuana plants?” Greg asked. He snorted and walked over to a sofa, slumped down and leaned forward to scoop up a marijuana pipe. The table was littered with papers, and bags of weed. “These towers smell like marijuana, day and night. No one is going to say shit. If they were, they would have said something by now.” He was starting to light up when Danny lunged forward and slapped it away from his mouth.

“They already have,” he said jabbing his finger towards the floor. “Your neighbor called city management to complain about blocked plumbing and large amounts of dog food found in her toilet. Turns out that dog food was pellets of grow medium, you dumb ass!”

Greg’s brow furrowed. “Oh shit, I thought that would flush away.”

“Well it didn’t. Now you need to get this out of here before…”

"Hold on. Hold on." Greg put up a hand and waved him off. "This is why you are here. You tell them it was a mistake. Nothing more than a mix-up. They'll believe you."

"Yeah, maybe they would if that was all." Danny rested his hand on his holster and shifted his weight from one foot to the next. "Did you sell any pot to anyone underage?"

"No."

"Oh so Mary-Anne's boy Tommy didn't get it from you?"

Greg moved around looking uncomfortable.

"Look, Danny, it was just a few bags."

"A few bags? His mother found fifty-eight grams of this shit under his bed."

Greg shrugged. "So? I gifted it to him."

"Gifted?" Danny spluttered.

"Yeah, the law says I can gift marijuana."

Danny squeezed his eyes shut trying to get a grip on his emotions before he went berserk and beat the living shit out of him. "That's to anyone over twenty-one. You idiot!"

"Shit." Greg ran a hand over his face and around the back of his neck.

"Yep, you're screwed. Now, maybe if you get rid of this now, you'll only end up doing five years."

His eyes widened. "Five years?"

"You gave him more than an ounce, Greg."

Greg wiped his lips with the back of his hand and walked over to the window. He glanced out across Prince William Sound, shaking his head. "But… but…"

"No buts. And while you're at it, call Cayden and tell him this agreement we have in place is over. It's done. If he wants the drugs, he's to come and get them himself."

Danny turned to walk out of the room.

Greg whirled around. "Hold on a minute, Danny. No, that can't happen."

"It will and it has. It's over. And we have you to thank for that. Chief Solomon already knows about Mary-Anne's boy. It's only a matter of time before he figures out the rest."

Greg stumbled over his furniture with a look of desperation in his eyes. "Cayden will kill us, and you know that."

"You mean you?" Danny said cutting him a glance.

"Screw you! You are in this as deep as I am," Greg said.

"Was. I'm out. You can tell him how you fucked up, or better still maybe I will."

Danny turned to walk away.

"Perhaps I'll tell him you did," Greg said. "Yeah, I'm sure he'd love that."

Danny stopped walking and cast a glance over his shoulder. He was about to go back and slap him a few times around the head when he noticed Greg was holding a revolver. He was holding it low but making the message real clear. Danny's own hand slid towards his service weapon but Greg shook his head. "I wouldn't if I was you."

He put out a hand. "Now hold on, Greg, you don't

want to do this."

"No I don't," he replied. "But you're not exactly giving me much choice. You knew what you were getting into when you signed up for this," Greg said tapping the revolver against his thigh.

"That was then. Before you attracted unwanted attention. Things have changed."

"Nothing's changed," Greg said jabbing his revolver forward at the floor. "So a neighbor complained, big deal! It was a mistake."

"And Tommy?" Danny asked.

"Make it go away." He frowned. "Like you always do."

Danny stared back at him. "No. You got sloppy this time, Greg. I'm not losing my career over this. Now get that shit out of here and I'll try to get the chief to go easy on you." He turned and started heading back towards the door when he heard a gun cock.

"Nah, this is how it's going to go," Greg said. "I'll get rid of the plants but you're going to deal with Solomon."

"Too late for that," Danny replied.

"So deal with him."

Danny's brow pinched together. "You better not be asking what I think you are."

"I'm not asking. I'm telling you. Deal with him or I will."

There were few relationships that mattered to Danny in Whittier, but his friendship with the police chief was one. He'd known Ed Solomon since he was ten years old, back when he wasted his days tearing around Begich Towers. Solomon had always treated him with respect. He hadn't just set the bar for what a police officer should be, he'd demonstrated genuine kindness. Danny looked up to him like a father figure. It was part of the reason why he didn't plan on staying in the game long. If Solomon ever learned of his involvement, it would destroy him. Hell, some days he wished he'd said no from the start. He'd been leery about getting involved since the beginning but he couldn't resist the extra money. Unlike many of the other police departments in Alaska, his salary was next to nothing. It certainly didn't afford him the lifestyle he wanted, the kinds of toys that rich folks had, or cover his drinking or gambling habit. That's why when Greg approached him, an old friend from back in his school days, he couldn't pass it up. Sure it went against everything he stood for as a cop but Greg was confident and reassured him it was just a short-time gig. Initially he turned him down but the seed of temptation had already been planted. Danny figured he could squirrel away enough from trafficking heroin that in a year he could retire. Well, it never happened. One year turned into another and before he knew it, here he was three years later, still a slave to the green.

Maybe if it hadn't been so damn easy he might have bailed, but the risk was low and no one questioned him. Greg had the whole operation running like a well-oiled machine. Heroin was brought in every two months like clockwork by a tourist on one of the cruise ships, he'd hand it off to Greg who would hold on to it until he could arrange a delivery date. From there Danny would place it in his cruiser and take it out of Whittier on his way home because unlike Solomon, he and the other six officers lived outside of the town and commuted in every day. It was simply a matter of exchanging money for the drugs and that was it. No one stopped or questioned them. It was why he'd stayed in so long. But that was before Greg screwed up.

"All right. Leave it with me," Danny said.

"Yeah?"

"You deaf?"

Greg didn't look convinced but after a few seconds he uncocked the gun and lowered it. A momentary lapse in judgment on his part. In one smooth move, Danny pulled his Glock 22. In the seconds that followed, he unloaded a round just as Greg reacted. Greg took the hit and tumbled back over a chair. Danny was about to press forward and finish him off but Greg was quick to return fire, wheeling the revolver around the chair and firing haphazardly. Danny darted into the bathroom to take cover and immediately got on the radio.

"Dispatch, shots fired. Shots fired. Requesting

backup."

More rounds lanced the doorway and tore into the concrete wall.

Danny reached up and with his elbow smashed the mirror and used a shard of it to get a bead on Greg. Nothing. Either he was still behind the sofa chair or had shifted position. Silence settled over the cramped apartment as he called out to him.

"Greg! You know this only ends one way."

"Screw you. If I go down, so do you," Greg said.

"The only way you are going down is with a bullet in the head," Danny replied.

He kept a firm hold on the grip of his gun as he twisted the shard of mirror around again to see if he could spot him. The tiny pot lights in the ceiling reflected off it, casting a reflection on the wall. Danny heard feet pounding across the living room area heading for one of the other rooms. Bringing his gun around he fired, once, then twice.

He missed.

More shots were returned.

In a town where you could go from one end to the other in less than five minutes, it didn't take long for backup to arrive. In the heat of the moment Danny hadn't heard the blare of sirens. There were only seven officers in the department, eight including the chief, and not all of them patrolled Whittier. A few of them headed out to Girdwood, and the rest assisted near the tunnel that provided access to Whittier through Maynard Mountain.

When he heard Solomon's voice his stomach dropped. He'd hoped Greg would be dead by the time they arrived but that slippery asshole had managed to evade.

"Danny?" Solomon asked.

Danny swallowed hard, breathed in deeply to calm down.

"Yeah, I'm here."

"You hit?"

"No."

"Open up."

The front door was closed. He knew he had to open it to let them in but once they were in, the situation would be out of his hands. Right now what they didn't see, they couldn't prove, and he'd already begun to work out what he would say.

Danny shifted position and tried one last time to see where Greg was. He crawled out into the narrow space between the bathroom and the living room and took a peek around the corner. The door was shut to the spare room. That asshole had barricaded himself in. Raising the Glock he fired four more times through the doorway in the hopes of hitting him but return fire confirmed he hadn't succeeded.

Banging began on the heavy fire door and he knew he couldn't delay the inevitable. Danny shuffled back to the front door and opened it to find Chief Solomon and two officers, Lucas Parker and Scott Black. Panting hard he thumbed over his shoulder as he stepped out into the corridor.

"Mitchell's barricaded himself in one of the rooms."

Solomon looked past him. "Why are you here?"

"Following up on the call we got."

"What call?"

"Not exactly a call." He brought him up to speed on what had led to his arrival, regarding grow medium blocking the pipes. "I came up here to talk to him. He was evasive, confrontational, and he pulled a gun on me…"

"That's not the truth!" Greg yelled from far back inside the apartment. Danny tried to close the door but Solomon wouldn't budge. Hoping to quell accusations before they occurred, he pushed his way back into the apartment and fired off another round.

"What the hell are you doing?" Solomon asked pulling him back. "He didn't fire at you."

"He tried to kill me."

"I meant right then," Solomon said.

There was a tense few seconds before Danny continued pointing to his spare room. "He has a grow op in there. At least twenty plants."

"Hey Danny, why don't you tell them about the heroin you've been trafficking!"

Solomon frowned and shot him a confused look.

"He's talking shit," Danny said before yelling back. "You better stop lying, you asshole!"

"Oh I ain't lying. Tell 'em about all those trips you made to Girdwood, to the drop-off."

"What is he on about, Danny?" Solomon asked.

The other two officers looked equally disturbed by the accusation.

"He's lying," Danny replied. At this rate Greg was going to screw everything up. In anger, he pushed past Solomon, and darted around the corner without a thought for his own safety, or the consequences of his actions. The only thought going through his mind was shutting Greg up. Danny kicked the bedroom door wide open, and even though Greg didn't have his weapon up, he yelled, "Police, drop it!" before unloading a round that ended his life. Only Danny was in far enough to see the real situation. Greg was clinging to a bloodied wound and sitting on the far side of the room with his revolver on the ground. One of the four shots he'd fired earlier must have struck him again, as he now had two gunshot wounds.

Danny gave him a third, straight through the heart.

When silence settled, Danny holstered his weapon, staggered out and slumped into a chair. Officer Black was the first one through the door. He stood there for a second and then said, "Chief, you should see this."

Solomon, who hadn't taken his eyes off Danny, made a gesture to Officer Parker to watch Danny as he entered the bedroom. A minute or two later he returned.

Danny looked down at his own feet, a million thoughts going through his mind, none of which were any good. Not only had he murdered his oldest friend in cold blood but he would now have to deal with the aftermath of questions.

"What did he mean, Danny?" Solomon asked directly.

He just shook his head. "No idea."

Solomon nodded, casting his eyes around the room. He told Black and Parker to tape it off, process the scene and not let anyone get inside. From there he took Danny out and they returned to the station. On the drive from the towers to the department Danny was quiet. "AIA will be called in for this, you know that, right?" Solomon said keeping his eyes fixed on the snowy road ahead.

Danny nodded.

Alaska Internal Affairs Department investigated incidents and suspicions of misconduct attributed to officers. This would be no different.

Solomon continued, "People will want answers. Greg's father will."

It was a close-knit community with less than two hundred people working in the town, which made it very hard for anyone to fly under the radar without someone knowing their business. How they had managed to get away with trafficking heroin this long without Greg opening his mouth was a miracle. Solomon continued asking him questions about what had happened but it just blurred together with the noise in his head. He felt like he was having an out-of-body experience. He felt removed from the situation. He didn't plan on killing him when he went in there. He thought Greg would understand. He thought Greg wanted to get out as much as he did — obviously not. Then there was Cayden Jones. He'd heard the rumors about him. The things he'd done to people who crossed him. The violence he'd inflicted on those who wanted to get out. Danny just figured he could talk his way out of it and use his position as a police officer to keep them at bay.

As the cruiser came to a stop outside the gray and blue, three-story Public Safety Building that housed police, fire and city offices and council chambers, he was already running the conversation he'd have with Cayden in his head.

Solomon turned in his seat.

"Listen, Danny. Is there anything you need to tell me? Because if there is, now would be the time."

He shook his head. A part of him wanted to speak up, and come out with it but the repercussions were too great. Solomon waited a few seconds, nodded and pushed out of the cruiser. They headed in and he told him to write up a report detailing everything that happened and then change out of his uniform and hand over his firearm and magazines as they would be taken as evidence. He would conduct an initial interview before a follow-up would be done a few days later. Just like most cops who shot someone in the line of duty, he would be placed on administrative leave until they had deemed the use of force was appropriate, at which time he would be allowed to return to active duty. These things were never easy. Officers were often forced to feel like villains for doing their job but it was the protocol, and although the town was small, and his relationship with Solomon was solid, he would be treated no different.

After filling out a short report, Danny passed by several administrative staff on the way to the locker room. They greeted him like it was just another day, but it wasn't. Nothing would be the same. He pushed into the changing room and took a seat on a wooden bench for a few minutes. Staring into space, he removed his duty belt and then looked at his service weapon. He wasn't thinking of Greg or what he would say to Solomon, or how he couldn't deviate from his story. He was thinking about Cayden, the drugs stashed away inside apartment 1003 and what would happen when he didn't make the drop.

He fished into his pocket for his cell. Although he had a number for his point of contact, he'd left the conversation and dealings to Greg. The only reason he agreed to get involved was on the basis that he had minimal involvement.

About to place the call, he heard a locker close and then saw an officer walk into view adjusting his duty belt.

"Oh, hey Danny."

"Sam," he replied.

The door swung closed, a gust of wind kicked up dust as he exited. Danny got up and checked that he was alone before placing the call. It would be the last time he made it. Satisfied that no one was there he tapped in the number and waited as it rang. His pulse sped up. A few seconds and a man he only knew as Vic answered.

"I need to speak to Cayden. It's about the drop."

"Hold on."

He heard voices; the sound of drilling then muffled chatter on the other end. Danny looked around nervously. He'd never placed a call to him from the department. He'd always done it from the burner phone in his SUV. But this was urgent. He had no idea how this was going to play out but it couldn't wait another day.

"Hello?" Cayden's grizzled voice answered.

"We got a problem."

"How big?"

"I can't make the drop."

"What?"

"Greg is dead. The cops are all over this. It's too hot."

There was a pause, long enough to make Danny think Cayden had hung up.

"Cayden."

A sigh. "They got my package?"

"No. But it's in a safe place inside the building."

"So bring it to me."

"I can't," Danny replied.

There was a noise behind him like a door closing. Danny put his hand over the phone receiver and backed up looking down the metal lockers that were separated by long wooden benches and a few feet. There was no movement. No sound. He returned to the conversation.

"Look, I need more time. I will get you the package but you'll have to wait."

"Wait?" The tone of his voice changed, deepening. "Yeah, that's not going to be good for business."

"It is what it is. Greg fucked up," Danny said.

"So clean up the mess and bring me my package, understood?"

"I got it. I'll bring it."

"Danny?" Solomon's voice echoed behind him. A shot of cold fear went through him as he hung up. He turned to face him like everything was good.

"Everything okay?" Solomon asked.

Danny gave a nervous smile. "Yeah. I guess."

Solomon drew closer and gave a nod. "Who was that?"

"What?"

"On the phone."

Danny lifted the phone. "Oh, just a friend."

"Yeah?" Solomon folded his arms and leaned against the end of the locker. "And has this friend got a name?"

Danny screwed up his face. "Look, I'll be out in a minute."

He stared back expecting Solomon to nod and walk out but he didn't. He remained there, stoic, unmoved and emotionless. "When is the drop happening?"

"What?" Danny asked.

"The package."

"That's nothing. Just—"

Solomon pushed away from the locker, his eyes narrowing. "Don't bullshit me."

"Ed, I don't know what you're on about."

"I heard you. Don't jerk me around."

"Look, chief. I mean, Ed."

Solomon put his hand out. "Hand over the phone."

"No. Why?"

"Hand it over."

"I have rights."

"So did Greg Mitchell. Now hand it over."

He felt pushed into a corner. He could have refused but in light of all that had happened and the accusations against him, he knew he didn't have a leg to stand on. He cursed under his breath as he handed it over. Solomon brought up the last number and redialed it. He never took his eyes off Danny for even a second. Although he didn't hear what was said on the other end, he'd heard enough.

"Hello?"

"Who is this?" Solomon asked.

The line went dead.

Solomon let out a heavy sigh and shook his head.

"How long have I known you, Danny?"

Danny navel gazed then looked up at him. "A long time."

If disappointment could be seen in someone's eyes, he

saw it in Solomon's that day.

"Why, huh? Why would you do this?"

Danny swallowed hard. There was no point lying any further. It was over. "Would it change anything if I told you?" he replied. Solomon clenched his jaw and his nostrils flared. "Ed, I didn't mean to. It was Greg. He..."

"Cut the shit," Solomon said. "I expected more from you."

Danny didn't reply.

"You don't deserve to wear that uniform."

"Ed, please. I..."

"Take the uniform off. After, you're going to show me where this package is."

"Then what?" Danny asked.

"You already know," Solomon said.

Danny shook his head. "Please, Ed, I won't last inside. You know what they do to cops. I'm begging you."

"Did Greg beg?"

"He pulled a gun on me first," Danny said.

Solomon cocked his head in disbelief so Danny

continued, "Whether you believe me or not. I know what happened."

"And you'll get plenty of time to tell us. Now get out of that uniform."

"You think I can take a shower first?"

"Get changed, Danny!" Solomon yelled.

"It's not like I'm going anywhere," he said looking around. There were a few small windows higher up to let in air but not large enough for an adult to climb out. Solomon nodded and told him he would wait for him and to hurry it up. Danny walked back and scooped up a towel along with his service weapon that was partially covered. He headed to the back of the locker room and entered the showers.

There he turned on the faucet and hot steam filled up the inside of the room and billowed out. Danny didn't bother slipping out of his uniform. He carried the Glock into the shower area and stood there for a second, holding it as warm water poured over his face and body. Salty tears mingled with the water and he regretted everything.

"You know, Ed, I'm really sorry I let you down."

There was no response. Hearing nothing was worse than the look of disappointment. It was over for him — his career, his reputation and his life, it was done.

He wouldn't survive a day inside the pen, and that's exactly where he was going. Danny raised the Glock to his temple, hesitated for a second then pulled the trigger.

Chapter 2

Two weeks later

Something didn't feel right. It was close to eleven fifteen at night when the red Ford SUV came to a crawl outside the Anton Anderson Memorial Tunnel. The radio played quietly in the background relaying news on the recent weather changes throughout the United States and the world. Over the past year there had been all manner of disasters: a major hurricane hitting Florida, a tsunami overwhelming the coast of Japan, earthquakes and wildfires on the West Coast. Up ahead, two vehicles were bumper to bumper with a large amount of snow on their roofs when Alex Riley eased off the gas behind them. He flipped his high beams on for a second. Snowflakes hovered among the evergreens in front of a snow-capped mountain. He squinted into the distance toward the triangular entrance to the tunnel that ran two-and-a-half miles through Maynard Mountain's rock. Steel shutters were down. It was closed? It couldn't be. It had been open when he'd arrived for his interview with the Whittier Police Department, two weeks ago. He didn't recall being told about a closure. Then again, thinking back to his fast-paced visit, it was all a bit of a blur. After doing three combat tours he'd returned to civilian life and had a hard time landing a job because he was infantry. He wasn't sure why but it was probably something to do with the fact that the skills that had been taught to him by the military weren't exactly transferrable. An employment specialist had told him he wasn't the first ex-soldier to struggle. Unsure of what he was well suited for, he opted for a career in the police.

Alex glanced at his family snuggled beneath blankets. The warmth of the vehicle had quickly lulled his wife and teenage kid into a slumber over the one-hour trip from Anchorage. He didn't want to wake them so he was careful to not make a noise as he pushed out into the wintry cold. Alex cut a glance back towards the booth they'd passed. It was unmanned. If there had been a sign for scheduled times he hadn't seen it. All he could recall from two weeks ago was them telling him that vehicles went through the single-lane passage every half an hour. Shivering, he stuck his hands into his puffy black jacket and jogged down to the car ahead of him. A thin layer of snow covered the windows. He looked inside and the driver appeared to be asleep. He tapped a few times on the window glass but he didn't respond. He continued on to the second. It was a 4 x 4 black truck, and the driver was lying with his head against a pillow pressed against the window. The truck was idling and kicking out a large plume of exhaust smoke. Alex blew into his cupped hands trying to warm them up. His breath expelled from his body like a ghostly apparition. It had to be around twenty degrees Fahrenheit. A quick knock on the glass and the driver stirred. He turned, Alex smiled, and the driver squinted at him. He could just make out his blurred face under the glow of the lights. The driver sat up and cracked the window. The guy had to be in his early fifties, a hard jawline, stubble, a full head of dark hair with a large amount of salt and pepper throughout.

"Can I help you?" he asked.

Alex jerked his head towards the tunnel. "Yeah, you know when the tunnel opens?"

"Five thirty in the morning."

"What?" He squinted. "But I've got to get into Whittier."

"You and me both. It closes at ten thirty every night."

"Why?"

"People need to sleep."

Alex frowned. "Well there must be another way in?"

"Yeah, by boat or plane. But I'm guessing you've got neither."

Alex blew into his hands. "This is insane."

The driver thumbed over his shoulder. "You should probably get back in your vehicle, sir. You're liable to freeze out here."

"Yeah, no shit. I knocked on the window of the guy behind you. He didn't respond."

"He's probably dead."

"What?"

"Happens all the time."

"All the time?"

The driver snorted. "It's a joke. Look, if you don't want to sleep in your vehicle, you might find a hotel back in Girdwood."

"But that's thirty minutes away," Alex said.

"It's either that, sleep here or head to Anchorage."

"That's where I just came from." He sighed rubbing his hands and trying to stay warm. "This is nuts. You planning on staying here the night?"

"Yep. Wouldn't be the first," the guy said.

"This happen often?"

"Yep."

Alex got a waft of his breath. He smelled like he'd been drinking.

"I can't believe they didn't tell me."

The guy stared at him for a second. "All the times are on the site."

"If you know that how did you end up getting locked out?" Alex asked.

"How do any of us get locked out?" the guy replied.

He didn't need to explain any further, and quite frankly Alex wasn't in the mood for chitchat. It was freezing outside and he was just pissed that no one had told him.

"It might help if they put up a sign or two."

"They have, you passed it back there." He snorted. "By the way, I'm Ed Solomon."

"The chief?"

Solomon nodded. "That'd be me."

"Alex Riley."

He burst out laughing. "Oh, the new hire. Right. Well that explains everything. Hold on, Debbie didn't tell you about the tunnel times?"

Now he felt like a complete fool. It wasn't even his first day on the job and he was already showing a lack of attention to details. He didn't want to throw anyone under the bus as there was a very good chance she told him in the middle of the hundreds of other things she conveyed. "Um. Maybe she did. To be honest I can't remember."

"Well at least you're honest. That goes a long way around these parts. Believe me."

Alex blew again into his hands. Solomon looked back at him.

"Listen, finding a room this late at night might be tough. I know the owner of one of the log cabins in Girdwood. He'll give me a good price, that is, if you folks are okay with sharing."

Alex tossed up a hand. "Oh, I don't want to put you out. We'll figure something out."

"Okay, but if you choose to stay in your vehicle, I would advise leaving the engine on for a while. You don't want to join dead guy back there," he said before chuckling and bringing up the window. Alex jogged back to his vehicle and hopped in. By now Jessica was awake.

"Are we here?" she asked.

He groaned. "Not exactly. Look, the tunnel is closed

for the night."

"Closed?"

"I know. I know."

"Alex, we just drove an hour. We can't sleep out here, we'll freeze to death."

He thumbed forward. "They're doing it."

She glared.

He tossed his hands up. "Okay!"

He looked on towards the chief's truck and scratched his head. At that moment his sixteen-year-old daughter Hayley woke up, looked out and then rolled back over again. Alex hopped out and hurried back to the truck and tapped on the window. Solomon brought it down.

"Change your mind or did the missus do that for you?"

Alex smirked. "If the offer is still open. We'd appreciate that."

"Not a problem. Follow me."

Chapter 3

The next morning, Alex's senses kicked into high gear with a strong coffee. Nursing his cup he glanced out the living room window and saw Solomon leaning against the front porch railing speaking on his cell. It was a little after seven. Beyond him, eight-foot snowdrifts had formed overnight, and the weather didn't appear to be letting up. The sky was overcast and a strong wind was picking up needles of snow and blowing it against the pane of glass. Both the truck and SUV had been swallowed by snow. They'd stayed the previous night in a gorgeous log cabin with a loft that held two beds, and a futon in the living room. It offered more than enough space, and with the wood-burning stove roaring away, it certainly beat sleeping in their vehicle at below-zero temperatures.

He glanced over his shoulder at the sound of feet. Jess emerged with a solid gray blanket wrapped around her, and thick red socks.

"Hey, darling, you want some coffee?" he asked.

She pawed at her eyes. "Sounds good."

Alex went back into the kitchen and poured out a cup while Jess took a seat at a table that looked as if it had been carved out of a redwood. Not long after he gave her a cup Hayley trudged in and plunked herself into a chair, pulling up her knees and wrapping her legs around her. Jess reached over and ran a thumb down her cheek. "You sleep okay?"

She nodded and glanced out the window at Solomon. "Is there anything to eat?"

"There's a granola bar in my bag if you want it," Jess said.

"I meant breakfast."

Jess looked over to Alex. He was about to say something when the front door opened and a huge gust of cold wind blew in. Solomon banged his boots on the bristled mat and shook off snow. "Whoa, it's getting crazy out there. Thinking we are in for one hell of a storm." He rubbed his hands together and looked at them. An awkward silence dominated. He hadn't said much the night before. All of them were tired and by the time they got the keys from the owner, they'd simply retreated to their respective beds. Solomon had opted for the futon, which Alex felt bad about. Here was his boss, and not only had his first time meeting him been an embarrassment, but now he felt indebted to the guy, even if they were splitting the cost of lodging.

"I'm really hungry," Jess said

"Me too," Solomon replied. "You know, there is a restaurant in town that does some mean pancakes but if you're really eager to get to Whittier, there's the Anchor Inn. It's good but it doesn't come close to the Girdwood Picnic Club. It's up to you?"

Alex said, "Don't you need to get back? I mean…"

He smiled. "There are six officers. We rarely get any trouble in Whittier, other than in the summer months when the odd tourist has had a little too much to drink. They'll be fine."

Alex nodded, then grimaced. "I dunno, I say we hit the

road before the weather gets worse and we get locked out again."

"But that's another thirty minutes," Hayley added.

"Actually, probably longer if we don't time it right. Traffic flows into Whittier every half hour," Solomon said walking past them and washing out his cup in the sink. "Then of course we have to take into account the weather."

Jess cocked her head. She didn't need to say anything, after eighteen years of being married he just knew the look.

He threw his hands up. "Okay. Pancakes it is."

Solomon winked at Hayley and she smiled back. In all honesty the thought of sitting around a breakfast table with his boss shooting the breeze and answering twenty questions wasn't how he saw his arrival in Whittier playing out. He was used to feeling his way out, observing from afar and getting a feel for what made each person tick. There was also the fact that he didn't want to be treated any different than the rest of the guys.

* * *

Surprisingly, Solomon didn't bombard him with questions when they arrived; he seemed too distracted by the waitress behind the counter. They soon came to learn that she was his ex-wife, Natalie, they'd been divorced for over two years but there was still some unfinished business between them. The restaurant was vibrant that morning with the sound of cutlery clinking, and the dinging of a bell when an order was ready. A guy and a girl in their late teens moved around the tables at a leisurely pace serving food and refilling cups with coffee.

As Solomon shoveled away a forkful of egg and bacon, he said, "Word of advice, if things ever get too much, leave Whittier. I should have twenty years ago but I was a fool." He washed his food down with a swig of coffee. "Lost a good woman because of it."

Alex glanced over at Natalie who was taking cash from a customer, then looked at Jess. He already knew what she was thinking because they'd had the conversation multiple times before he took the job. She didn't want to be there but after the loss of their second child two years ago, he didn't have much choice. It was the reason he'd left the military. Their youngest was only eight when he came down with influenza. The sudden onset was unexpected and aggressive. Alex was away from home at the time and Jess had to deal with it alone. She did all the right things but it was out of her hands. The loss of their son almost destroyed their marriage, and sent Jess into a downward spiral. She quit her job as a nurse and he'd been trying to balance work and personal life since then, and, if he was honest, it had all started to become a little too much. Even though the military had been accommodating there was only so much they could do. Eventually he had to reevaluate his work so he could be closer to home. Within a matter of months of being discharged he went through the process to become a cop. While some might have said that was the worst career move he could have taken, it was the only one that allowed him to use the skills he'd gained. Landing a position in Anchorage was another thing entirely. It was a lengthy and competitive process and one that didn't pan out. That's when he spotted the posting for a full-time officer in Whittier. It seemed almost too good to be true, the timing, the speed of hiring and an apartment in Begich Towers.

"Mr. Solomon, you mind me asking why your wife left?" Jess asked.

Alex was quick to jump in, "Jess. I don't think he..."

"Ah, it's okay. It's a valid question." Solomon took another swig of his drink, then picked out some food between his teeth before answering, "A lot of people come to Whittier for different reasons. Some enjoy being social, others want to be left alone. Not everyone stays. Not everyone can deal with the isolation. If you're not very stable it can send a person over the edge."

Jess tossed Alex a look and he tried to act like he wasn't paying attention by tucking into his pancakes.

"So why did you stay?" she asked.

He shrugged, glancing over to Natalie. "She'd say I was stubborn and she'd be right but Whittier has a way of getting into your blood. You either love it or hate it but there is no denying it's a beautiful place. You'll see."

"Is it true the town is all under one roof?" Hayley asked.

He smiled. "Somewhat. In fact it's one of the most common questions we get asked. There are a lot of rumors swirling around but the truth is about ninety percent of the town live in Begich Towers, the rest commute or live in a small condo on Blackstone Road. Interestingly enough and you may not have known about this but for the longest time the police department, city hall, the town school, the general store, the post office, the pharmacy, and medical clinic were all inside the towers until recently."

"All?" Hayley asked sounding surprised.

"Yep but recently the clinic, police department, and city hall moved to a brand-new building about a minute away. It's probably for the best as months could go by and some residents wouldn't venture out at all. Then you had people coming in at all hours of the day asking the dumbest questions."

"Why?" Hayley asked.

"People are dumb?"

"No I mean, why didn't they venture out?"

"There was no need to. Everything you needed was there. Of course some folks chose to travel to Anchorage once a month to stock up on groceries but beyond that unless your job calls for you to head out, people stay inside."

"But all the rest is still there. The school?" Jess asked.

"Yep. There's a tunnel in the basement that heads over to the school. It's cool. It's what makes Whittier unique. You'll see. I think you'll like it."

"What if I don't?" Hayley asked.

Alex nearly choked on his bacon. He reached for some orange juice to wash it down. Hayley was so downright honest.

"You okay there?" Solomon asked before chuckling.

He gasped as he caught his breath. "Yeah, food just went down the wrong way." Alex glanced at Hayley and narrowed his eyes hoping she would understand his non-verbal communication.

"So you got any kids yourself, chief?" Alex tried to change the subject.

"Call me Ed," Solomon replied. "And yeah, one boy, he's twenty-two, works in Anchorage. Fortunately he had the good sense to stay clear of policing and land himself a job in the tech industry. I see him from time to time but for the most part we talk by phone."

"So you on speaking terms?" Alex asked.

Solomon cut a glance towards Natalie.

"I am, she's not," he replied tossing a napkin on his plate. "You could say things didn't exactly end well. I can't fault her. In fact I'm surprised she stuck around as long as she did."

"She fall in love with someone else?" Hayley blurted out.

"Hayley," Jess said in a reprimanding way.

Her eyebrows shot up. "Just a question. Geesh."

Solomon chuckled. "I wish it was that easy, but no,"

he replied looking over at her with longing in his eyes. "Sometimes people just drift apart."

Alex followed his gaze and Natalie looked their way.

"But you still love her?" Hayley asked.

Alex scowled as Solomon replied, "Yes. Very much." He got a pained expression on his face. "Anyway, we should head out. Looks like it's getting bad out there."

The flakes were falling even heavier than before. It was getting hard to see because of the wind. A loud snowplow rolled past curling up snow to one side of the road.

"Yeah, right. Look, I'll cover this," Alex said sliding out.

Solomon threw up a hand. "No, I'll pay."

"After what you did last night, it's the least I can do."

"All right, thanks."

As Alex lined up behind two other people who were paying their bills, a flat-screen behind the counter played out a news broadcast. A red ticker along the bottom was alerting them to winter storm warnings all along the coast of Alaska. He couldn't hear what was being said as the volume was low but it didn't look good. It wasn't like anything was new, over the past three years the weather had been doing all manner of unusual things, all of which seemed to be ramping up for what some were calling a superstorm. In front of him two guys were muttering about how damn cold it was, and they were sure the government was behind it. Alex chuckled. Conspiracy theorists looked for any reason to blame it on anyone else. Of course it didn't matter whether it was hot or cold, people just loved to complain. A waitress behind the counter started surfing through the channels trying to find something less depressing. Several of the national stations were reporting on global weather at the top of the hour, replaying some of the unusual events that had occurred over the past year. On the screen, catastrophic weather played out before their eyes with Istanbul being hit by golf ball-sized hail and ferocious winds that spun a hotel lobby's rotating door wildy on its own. It then switched to wildfires, which had broken out across Australia, and California in the summer from a heat wave, through to five hurricanes hitting the East Coast and causing significant casualties. Then there were the devastating floods in India, Pakistan, Nepal, and Bangladesh causing over a thousand deaths. Home videos sent in by viewers showed vehicles veering out of control on the highways in Europe after what they were calling the heaviest and deadliest snowstorm in decades. It quickly shifted back to America, and reports of snow, freezing rain and ice covering much of the state of Texas, before it switched to incredibly dark twisting tornadoes tearing across California wreaking havoc and destroying everything in their path. The waitress shook her head and switched again to what looked like an interview with a climatologist. He was answering questions on the unusual weather events over the past few years, how climate change could affect the weather, and what was being done to support contingency planning.

"Well Tracey, let me start by making clear the difference between weather and climate change. It all comes down to timing. The weather is the conditions we are seeing in the atmosphere over a short period of time, while climate is how the atmosphere behaves over a longer period of time. So when I'm talking about climate change, I'm speaking about the changes in average temperatures, rainfall, etc. Basically, once you understand the role climate change has played in heat waves, wildfires, droughts, extreme flooding, snowstorms, and what causes these, such as the ocean and atmospheric patterns of warming and cooling, we can better prepare ourselves for a big weather event."

Tracey nodded. "Interesting. So with all the rough weather the country has been having lately, do you foresee a big event? I mean folks are talking about a superstorm on the horizon. It that possible?" she asked.

"It's very possible and we are carefully monitoring changes."

Tracey jumped back in. "Which brings up the question, what causes these? How much does global warming play a role in driving these deadly events? And could we be looking at a new mini ice age?"

"Good question. Well, temperatures certainly play a big role in the weather we experience. It's no mystery that industry and burning fossil fuels are related to the extreme events we've been seeing around the world. The fact is despite the climate policies we have in place, solar advances, use of wind farms, hybrid cars, and campaigns to cut down on global warming... greenhouse gas emissions are still moving us in the wrong direction."

Tracey's brow furrowed. "I'm confused. I thought we were doing a good job?"

"We are. Well some of us are. Look, I don't want to point fingers but in the last year we have seen an estimated two percent rise driven by pollution in China and India, offsetting the good work being done in the United States and other countries."

"So one step forward, and two back."

"Exactly," he replied. "Unless our global climate efforts are on the same page we don't stand a chance of slowing down the inevitable."

"Which is?" Tracey asked.

"A superstorm climate shift that would affect the world on a devastating scale — essentially taking us beyond a point of no return. My concern is that we are at that tipping point already."

Tracey nodded. "So as the planet warms we would see rising sea levels, a disintegration of polar ice sheets and coastal flooding, right?" she asked.

"Exactly. Except it would make Superstorm Sandy, which narrowed New Jersey's beaches by more than thirty feet, look like child's play. Hell, back then some folks lost electricity for a few days, and heat and hot water for more than two months. That's nothing to what is coming."

The interviewer looked worried. "So mass evacuations?"

He scoffed. "If there's time. The problem is, Tracey, humanity is not prepared."

"Why?"

"Because we're not aware of the gravity of the situation before us. Let's face it, we live in a bubble of ignorance at what is happening around us. TV shows, celebrity news and social media all play a role in dumbing us down. And with busy lives, and misinformation being spouted, we can barely see past our own noses. Unfortunately we assume if all is well in our backyard, our town and our state — we don't need to worry about what is happening beyond that. Heck, the government will come in and save the day, right? Wrong. We need to be concerned and mindful and take the necessary steps before it's too late." He shook his head and continued. "Need? The fact is the damage has already been done. We have dramatically altered this planet by choosing to be a fossil fuel-driven civilization. The flooding, the droughts, the wildfires, the cyclone bombing, these were just the beginning. Like an achy tooth before it breaks."

"You make it sound like we are already over the tipping point."

The climatologist paused and put a finger up to his ear as if he was hearing someone speak to him through his earpiece. He grimaced, nodded and answered the news anchor. "What I'm saying is unless a joint effort is made across the globe we aren't looking at centuries, or even decades before the next devastating climate shift occurs, it will be sooner."

"How soon?" she asked.

The TV screen started going fuzzy, white noise took over and the image of the two people was barely visible. The waitress reached up and hit the screen a few times but it didn't seem to do anything. She flipped through channels then gave up.

"Damn storm!" she said switching it off.

By now those in front of Alex had finished and he stepped forward to pay.

Chapter 4

In a dusty warehouse in the city of Anchorage, Cayden Jones, otherwise known as "Bullet" on the streets, sat behind a mahogany desk snorting a line of coke. He rubbed his nose with two fingers and inhaled deeply as he rocked his head back. It had become a habit way back in the day when he was a small-time dealer. Everything had to be checked, no one trusted anyone and testing the goods was critical.

A lot had changed in twenty years. At the age of thirty-nine he had finally established himself as the go-to man for high-end drugs on the streets. He'd clawed his way to the top using violence to instill fear and establish his territory. Anyone who caused problems was dealt with immediately. There could be no room for error. One slight oversight and his whole world could come crashing down. He hadn't worked this many years to see it crumble.

Compared to the way things were ten years ago, business had been good. He rarely showed his face unless it was required. In his profession, he counted the money, gave orders and oversaw the day-to-day operations. He let those that worked for him take the risks. It was easier that way. Then again he wasn't one to shy away from taking matters into his own hands if required. But those days were far and few between now.

The sound of an industrial sander cut through the silence.

When he wasn't cutting deals and distributing, he ran an auto body shop in the downtown, as well as a series of online gambling sites. Of course it was all smoke and mirrors for where the real money was being made but it gave him a way to launder money, and stay under the radar. He looked up at the opaque glass that wrapped his second-floor office. Through the window he could just make out Vic standing outside the door waiting for him. He was one of four he trusted, a close inner circle of friends that had stuck close since the early days.

"Vic," he called out.

Vic entered. He was a large guy with a bald head. He wore a leather jacket, dark jeans and combat boots. Cayden couldn't begin to count the number of people's faces that had his boot print embedded in their skin. "Yeah?"

"Is he here yet?"

Vic shook his head.

Cayden nodded. "So he's gonna be a no-show."

"Seems that way. You want us to pay him a visit?" Vic asked.

"No, I'll do it," Cayden said. He sniffed hard as he rose.

"All right, I'll get the boys together."

"Don't bother. I'll handle this one."

Cayden moved across the office, stopping only to put on his winter jacket, and collect a set of brass knuckles from a drawer. He glanced in the mirror and ran his fingers through his dark hair. It was swept to one side, fashionable with a little gel. He liked to look good, appearances were everything. He pulled at the skin below his green eyes. He needed more sleep. Too many late nights were beginning to catch up. He wiped away some remaining powder under his right nostril, and stepped out onto the metal catwalk that ran along the upper level of the warehouse. Vic closed the door behind him.

Below, several sedans and SUVs were being worked on. Dust rose in the air inside an enclosed room above a '57 Chevy that was being sanded. Farther down a truck was in the middle of a repaint job. It was business as usual. Nothing out of the ordinary. As Cayden made his way down the steps, he said, "Any word back from Leon on the package?"

"I phoned an hour ago but couldn't get through. Damn weather is affecting service."

"Well let's hope he manages to collect it."

Before he made it to the ground, Hank entered the building with Terry Hammond, the man he was about to pay a visit. Cayden gave him a stern look but didn't say a word. He leaned over and whispered into Vic's ear and

Vic nodded and crossed the room to tell those working on vehicles to stop and leave. They were used to it. A few seconds later, and the sander turned off and silence dominated.

"Hey, Bullet," Terry said looking around nervously as workers left the warehouse, and Hank slid closed the main doors and locked them.

"You know for a moment I thought you weren't going to show."

Terry chuckled nervously, his eyes bounced between Vic and Cayden. "Me? No. You said to come here and so here I am."

"And here you are," Cayden replied sniffing the air like a dog. He prowled around him like a lion watching its prey. Cayden nodded slowly saying nothing. He enjoyed the silence. He knew those who liked to talk a lot, and get theatrical when dealing with someone who had screwed up, but that wasn't him. No, he enjoyed letting them sweat. Making them wonder what he was thinking. In fact he relished it more than the punishment he inflicted.

Though he had gained a reputation for bloodshed, he preferred not to inflict pain. It was uncalled for, and yet at times necessary. This was one of those times.

"Look, Bullet, the cops were everywhere. I had no choice."

He walked over to the room with the Chevy and looked through the window. Dust had attached itself to the window, and settled on the ground. One of his workers had stripped the original paint off and was getting it ready for a new paint job.

"So you flushed it?" Cayden asked.

"I had no choice. It was that or get caught and do time. And you know, they would eventually trace it back to you and well I was doing it to protect you."

"Protect me?"

Terry nodded, a smile forming on his face as if he'd managed to find an angle, a way to make his fuck-up more palatable. It had the reverse effect.

"And why would I need protecting when you're the one doing the selling?" Cayden asked.

"Yeah but…"

"Unless of course you were planning on ratting."

Terry threw up his hands. "Oh no. No, Bullet. I wouldn't do that. You know me. That's not my way."

"No?"

Cayden stood with his back to him, looking at his reflection in a pane of glass. He reached into his pocket nice and slowly and slid on the brass knuckles, allowing a moment to feel the cold metal wrap around his fingers. Beautiful.

"Then how would they trace it back to me?" he asked running his other hand over the hard metal.

"Well. Um. You know how the police are good at shaking people down."

"Getting people to speak, you mean?"

"Yeah."

"So you would tell them?" Cayden asked.

"No. I flushed the drugs so I wasn't put in that position."

"But if you were in that position?"

"I…" He stumbled over his words, realizing the error of his ways. In his attempt to try and cover his ass he'd made it clear what he would have done had he been caught. It was a risk that Cayden had to take. Even though he went by the name Bullet on the streets and rarely gave out his address or showed his face, there was always a chance the cops might eventually find him and that was why he'd already formulated an exit plan. He only intended to stay in the drug business another couple of years. Once he had another ten million stashed away he was going to retreat to somewhere warm, somewhere far from Alaska, and live out the remainder of his days chugging back beers and enjoying a life far from the dangers of his world. Leon, his closest friend, had been harping on at him for over a year to call it quits, and he was right. The truth was it was becoming harder to stay one step ahead of the police. Of course he had a few cops on the payroll, those who were willing to give him the heads-up, if and when a raid ever occurred. And he'd made sure to have collateral on them in the form of video just in case they decided to grow a conscience.

It was all about control, or perceived control.

Cayden turned towards him, expressionless.

"How are you going to pay me back, Terry?"

Terry frowned, a look of confusion. "Pay you?"

"Yeah. I mean you were responsible. How do I know you didn't just sell it and keep the profits?"

"Because I wouldn't do that to you."

"And yet you just said if you had been taken in, they would trace it back to me."

"That's not what I meant. I…"

He knew what was coming, they all did. His reputation preceded him. Over the years, stories of what he'd done to those who crossed him continued to be twisted and exaggerated but even when they were true, one thing remained the same — blood was shed, and a bullet was fired.

Cayden nodded, smiled ever so slightly as he laid a hand on Terry's shoulder, and patted him. "It's okay."

Terry blinked hard. "Yeah?"

He nodded, glanced once at Terry and then drove the brass knuckles into his stomach before following through with an uppercut that knocked him to the ground. Terry gasped, and clutched his stomach but Cayden wasn't finished. He bent over and clasped a clump of his hair and dragged him a few feet across the concrete floor into the room with the industrial sander. All the while Terry was trying to spit out words but all that escaped his lips were choked sounds. Cayden dragged him up onto the hood of the vehicle, and gestured to Vic and Hank to hold him down while he tore open Terry's shirt. Terry struggled to get free but it was pointless. His legs flailed around and he screamed out for mercy but he was beyond that point now. Without rushing, Cayden walked over to the industrial sander and scooped it up.

"Now look at what you're making me do."

"Please! Bullet, I'm sorry. I'll get the money."

Cayden turned and said, "No you won't."

He fired up the sander, returned and slammed it down on Terry's chest.

* * *

Five minutes later, Cayden walked out of that room, his clothes soaked in blood. He tucked his Beretta into the small of his back and headed to his office to change his clothes. Behind him, Vic and Hank went about cleaning up the mess, and disposing of the body.

As he was trudging up the stairs, the phone rang, and he answered.

It was Leon. The reception was poor. It crackled.

"Leon? Speak up!" he yelled as he put a bloodstained finger into his ear so he could hear him better.

"There's been a hiccup."

"Oh?"

"The cop is dead. Apparently he took his own life." Cayden stopped walking and stood at the top of the catwalk looking out across the warehouse. It had been almost two weeks since his conversation with Danny. That pig had reassured him he'd have the package. He needed that load, he relied on the system he'd set up. Without a way to get the drugs into Alaska his business would soon dry up. For years he'd been buying it from another dealer on the East Coast and having it brought across the country by long-distance truckers but that process was slow and it ate into his profit margin. Once he found a way to cut out the middleman and get it directly using cruise ships that entered the port of Whittier, his business had soared to new heights. It was the perfect cover.

Leon piped up. "Cayden. What do you want me to do?"

"We'll figure out the logistics for the next shipment later, for now just bring back the package."

"That's the thing. It's not there."

"What?" He felt his stomach drop. It wasn't the loss of heroin that bothered him. Even though that could be replaced, it was the timing and loss of clients. He didn't just cater to two-bit street addicts; he serviced high-end clientele who paid in advance. They relied upon delivery of goods and he hadn't failed them yet. But this? This could ruin him. It could do more than set him back a few months; it could jeopardize everything he'd built. Trust was all he had in this business. Once that was gone so was everything else.

"Check his apartment," Cayden said.

"I searched Greg's apartment. It's empty."

He shook his head and began pacing. "No. It can't be."

"Maybe he put it in another one," Leon said.

"Shit!"

"What should I do?"

He was tired of leaving this in the hands of others.

Cayden grit his teeth. "Nothing. I'm coming down."

Chapter 5

The blizzard made visibility brutal. Jess and Hayley gawked out the windows as they came out of the two-and-a-half miles of dark tunnel and took in the sight of an overcast Whittier. To the right, the White Mountains loomed over the cramped town on three sides, adorned with snow-brushed evergreens, trails and frozen waterfalls. Rosy-cheeked kids trudged through the deluge, others peered out from behind panes of glass. On the left was Prince William Sound, a bay of blue that never froze because of its deep waters. Hired hands shoveled globs of snow off docked vessels. At the center of the town, nestled at the foot of the mountain, stood the remarkable fourteen-story building, Begich Towers; a huge, somber high-rise painted in beige, light blue and gray. Surrounding it, nothing more than small aged buildings, train lines, shacks, kayak rentals, harborside eateries and two inns. Beyond that, at the far edge of town, the

Buckner Building stood out, a hulking gray concrete monolith, seven stories high, that had been abandoned since the army bailed in the sixties. Solomon had been filling them in on the place over breakfast. Apparently it was used by the military and dated back to the '50s, containing a hospital, a theater, a bowling alley, a jail, a rifle range, a bakery, a lounge, a library and much more.

Alex brought the SUV to a stop outside Begich Towers. Solomon collected the key to their apartment and said he would meet up with Alex later for a drink at the Anchor Inn. He said he would go over some things he needed to know and if they had any questions in the meantime to speak to Kip Brown, the owner of the Kozy Korner grocery store in the building. According to Solomon, Kip considered himself a pillar in the community, but to most he was just the town drunk.

"Well here we are, the end of the road," Alex said.

"The end of the road? You're telling me, this place sucks," Hayley said holding up her cell trying to get a signal. "Does it even have internet?"

"Of course," he said.

"What, dial-up or carrier pigeon?"

"Hilarious. Come on, help us lug in some baggage."

Alex pushed out of the vehicle and gazed at two penned-in reindeer. It truly was a world apart from the big city, or the sweltering deserts of the Middle East. Once they made their way inside and shook off the snow, they ascended a small series of steps to a lobby that looked as bland as the outside with institutional-pale yellow concrete walls, uniform green doors and low-end carpeting throughout. Immediately off to their right was a small waiting area, with a couple of wooden benches and an old woman who was curled up in a fetal position. Hayley raised an eyebrow then continued on to the elevators. Alex was beginning to regret taking the position. They walked on down the hallway past a laundromat where someone had dumped a pile of clothes on the ground. Rusted washing machines dating back to the '80s churned loudly, shaking uncontrollably while a withdrawn-looking resident looked on absently like a mental patient.

"This place gives me the creeps," Hayley said stepping into the elevator and hitting the button for the tenth floor. As the doors clunked closed Alex noticed there was no thirteenth floor. Before he said anything, Hayley said, "Okay now that's just abnormal. Ten, eleven, twelve, fourteen, fifteen. What happened to thirteen?"

"It doesn't exist," Alex said.

"Of course it does."

"No, it's quite common, actually. In some hotels they will make the thirteenth floor the pool floor, or some just leave it out completely. It's something to do with a disorder called triskaidekaphobia," Jess said.

"She means they're superstitious," Alex added. "Apparently the practice of removing the thirteenth floor is to avoid alienating superstitious clients."

Hayley shook her head. "This place just keeps getting weirder. Dad, couldn't we have bought a place outside of Whittier? Chief Solomon said that barring himself the other officers commute in. Why can't you do that?"

"Because."

"Because what?"

"Because this was more affordable and practical."

Hayley looked dumbfounded. "I'm not sure having a building with no thirteenth floor is practical."

He rolled his eyes as they arrived at their level and stepped out. Several kids hurried past wearing pajama bottoms and thick winter jackets. They were followed by a mother who had nothing on her feet.

"Doesn't anyone get dressed?" Hayley asked.

Alex ignored the question as they arrived at apartment 1003. Across from them he stared at yellow police tape dangling in front of apartment 1002. It looked as if someone had torn through it.

Jess noticed too. "That doesn't look good."

He waved her off. "Ah it's fine."

"You think someone was murdered in there?" Hayley asked.

He didn't answer; instead he inserted the key and pushed the door to their apartment open. Hayley darted in eager to be the first inside. It had been something she'd done ever since she was little, however, that was usually in nice hotels where everything was fancy, modern and worked.

She came to a grinding halt and flipped the light switch up and down. "The lights don't work," she said.

"Probably the weather," Alex replied.

Even though it was daylight outside, it was so overcast that it was dark in the apartment. Jess dumped the bags and entered the open kitchen. She began opening cupboards. "Nice, it comes fully furnished."

Alex came up behind her and wrapped his arms around her waist and nuzzled his mouth into the crook of her neck. "I told you. We've got it made."

"Oh yeah, we've got it made," she said sarcastically after turning on the faucet. It spluttered to life kicking out Coke-colored water. They both grimaced.

"Probably just needs to run through," he said.

They watched it run for a couple of minutes without getting clearer.

Alex sighed. "I'll speak to maintenance."

She tapped him on the chest. "You do that and while you're at it maybe you can ask if they will move us into another apartment — the penthouse for instance."

"You are kidding?"

"About the penthouse, yes, but Solomon said they've got 196 apartments. Surely there is one that is in a better state than this."

"Maybe, but remember the top two floors are taken up with mostly rentals for the bed and breakfast," he replied crouching down and getting under the sink, hoping to see if there was a quick way to fix it, only to discover a leaky pipe. He closed the doors before Jess saw it.

"Hey, well at least they have TV," Hayley said plunking herself down on the sofa and snatching up the clicker. She switched it on only to find it hissing with white snow. "Please tell me you got it hooked up?"

He grimaced. "First thing on Monday."

"Monday?" she groaned and switched off the TV.

Alex came over and sat beside her and nudged her in

the ribs. "I promise things are going to work out just fine here. You'll see. Heck, you might make friends with those kids we saw."

"Yeah, and maybe I'll get a lobotomy while I'm at it," Hayley replied. Alex laughed and tickled her ribs. She stifled a laugh then shook her head.

"Dad, get off. I'm not eight anymore." She jumped up and went to explore the rest of the cramped apartment. It was a 1,200-square-foot abode with three bedrooms, one bathroom and a kitchen with large windows that gave them a view of Whittier Harbor, the mountains, cruise ships and the ferry terminal.

"Uh, Alex."

"Oh no, what now?"

"I think we might have a leaky pipe."

He fumbled with the clicker and leaned back on the sofa. "Under the sink. I know."

"Under the sink? No, I meant in the main bedroom."

His stomach sank. He hopped up and went to take a look. Sure enough, one of the ceiling tiles had a stain. He reached up and noticed it was dry. "Actually I think we're good. It's probably just from a while back. Feels good to me."

"That might have mildew," Jess said.

"I'll get them to look at it. Okay?"

He headed for the door to see if he could track down Kip or at least give his mind a mental break. As he came out, he pushed back against the door as two kids raced down the corridor.

"Get back here, you brats!" a guy in his sixties said. He glanced at Alex and smiled before hurrying after them. Welcome to Whittier, Alex told himself as he headed for the elevator. All the doors in the place were painted the same. The only difference was some had an anchor door knocker, or a wreath, and on one he saw a notice of an exterminator's next scheduled visit. Was the place infested? He tapped impatiently a few times and glanced up and down the corridor. There were four elevators and two stairwells, and while the building itself was one large tower, it was divided into three parts, a purposeful design that was done to ensure it could withstand an earthquake. Stepping into the elevator he felt like a fish out of water. On the way down he tapped his fingers against the steel and looked up at the mirrored elevator ceiling tiles. What are you doing here? he mulled. Maybe Jess was right, perhaps he had been too hasty in taking the offer. There was a chance he could have landed a job with one of the other cities in Alaska if they didn't have bills to pay. But without Jess working, all the pressure was on him to provide and he didn't have the luxury of waiting.

As the doors to the elevators opened, three unsavory-looking guys squeezed past him. Alex turned back for a second and one of them grinned at him before the doors closed.

An uneasy feeling washed over him. Alex pushed it out of his mind and headed on down the hallway to locate the Kozy Korner. The door was slightly ajar and on the wall it listed the scheduled open hours. Alex pushed in to find an old guy with a huge white beard doing squats while holding a broomstick over the back of his shoulders with two cans of household paint dangling off the ends. If that wasn't strange enough, he was wearing a sleeveless AC/DC T-shirt, tight black shorts and construction work boots.

"Fifty-seven, fifty-eight, fifty-nine."

"Hello," Alex said.

The old-timer ignored him, focusing on his reps and breathing. Alex noticed a familiar tattoo on his arm. It was of a bulldog and below it had the letters U.S.M.C. The United States Marine Corps. Down the back of his weathered-looking calf muscle was the phrase SEMPER FIDELIS.

"Sixty-one, sixty-two."

"Um, Ed Solomon told me to see you if there were any problems."

"Sixty-four, sixty-five."

Alex raised an eyebrow and surveyed the room. It was cramped with stacked shelving containing all types of canned and bottled foods. There was a small desk with a cash register and laptop, various types of fruit, muffins and cereal stacked up in front of it. Behind the counter two shelves were full of old and new DVDs. There was even a small blackboard with the names of five new releases, and Kip's recommended movies — *Apocalypse Now,* and *The Deer Hunter.* A shelf to the right of that had a few packs of smokes, some chewing tobacco, lighters, vape juice, and several boxes of condoms, batteries, lip balm, and playing cards. Beyond that was a small blue washroom with a bucket and mop, and leaning against the wall was a bolt-action rifle. It was odd to see it out in the open like that. He might have said something if he was in uniform but with being new and all, and having no idea how things worked around here, he opted to say nothing.

Alex jerked a thumb over his shoulder. "My family and I just moved into apartment 1003."

"Seventy-eight."

"Yeah, seems we have a leaky faucet, the TV might be on the blink, and uh… one of the lights is blown."

No response, he continued. "You uh… going for some

world record there, old-timer?"

The old man paused in the middle of a squat and glanced at Alex, looking him up and down before finishing off with a few more squats.

"Ninety-eight, ninety-nine, one hundred."

He tossed the wooden bar back, letting it hit the floor and clatter, then he rose. For someone of his age he was in good shape.

"So you're the new kid Solomon hired?"

"That's right."

He sized him up and cracked his head to both sides and did this thing with his jaw that made it sound like it was unhinging. He walked around his desk and sat down and tapped at his computer mumbling under his breath. Alex assumed he was checking some kind of schedule or looking something up. He twisted in his seat, stuck a pair of spectacles on the end of his nose and turned on a small radio, extending the antenna before twisting the knob until he landed on weather.

"So you think you can come and take a look?"

"Later."

"How much later?"

He peered over his specs. "You city folk."

"What's that mean?"

He snapped his fingers a few times. "Everything has to be now."

"Well it would be good to be able to see."

"It's daylight."

"But it will eventually be evening and let's face it, this place doesn't appear to get much sunshine."

"It gets enough."

"Oh yeah?"

"We had eleven eight-hour days of sunshine last year."

"Wooh, let's throw a party," he joked, thinking that Kip would laugh. He didn't. His eyes narrowed and turned back to what he was doing which appeared to be absolutely anything else but coming and checking out the apartment issues.

"Anyway, you'd probably be best off with a flashlight," Kip said.

"What?"

He motioned towards the shelf where there were two.

"Oh right, for now," he said leaning forward and picking one up. "Thanks."

"That'll be forty bucks."

"What?"

"For the flashlight."

"But you said..." Then he clued in. "Okay then, maybe I'll just figure out the problem myself. You want to direct me to where the fuse box is?"

"You probably just need a new bulb." He pointed to a box on the counter. Alex frowned growing a little tired of his subtle sales pitches.

"Look, man, do you think you can come take a look?"

"I'm not in charge of maintenance. That's a different department."

"Of course it is." He rolled his eyes wondering why he'd spent the last five minutes going back and forth with him. "Well, would you mind pointing me in the right direction?"

"I would but Dougy, the guy who's in charge, is away. Yeah, on vacation in Hawaii, lucky bastard."

"So who do I speak to?"

"Well that would be me."

Alex reached up and squeezed the bridge of his nose feeling a headache coming on. Before he could find the words to say how utterly confused he was, Kip jumped up and laughed. "I'm just shitting with you. Of course I'll take a look. We don't get many new folks around these parts, and I just couldn't resist." He got up and picked up a toolbox from underneath his desk and headed over to the door. "Well come on then, lead the way."

They stepped out and he locked up and turned over a sign that said, "Back Later."

"Aren't you going to be a little cold?" Alex asked, pointing out the obvious.

That only made him laugh hard. "You city folks. This isn't cold. You wait until the storm of the century hits."

"The what?" Alex asked falling in step and trying to keep up. For a man of his age, Kip was one peppy little guy.

"The storm. Haven't you been following the news? Hell, take a look outside."

His mind flashed back to the TV in the restaurant that morning.

"Oh that."

"Yeah, that." He shook his head. "This is going to be the big one. I've been telling folks around here for the last four years but will they listen? Nope." He stepped into the elevator and tapped the tenth floor button. The steel jaws sealed closed, and the elevator lurched upward.

Chapter 6

The phone rang as Ed Solomon slipped into his police uniform. He scooped it up and answered. "Yeah go ahead," he said as he continued adjusting his tie. It was the AKRR dispatch in Anchorage.

"Chief, we have to shut the tunnel early due to the weather. It's just too bad out there."

"What?"

He walked over to the window to take a look. Sure enough, it was a complete whiteout, heavy winds battered the public safety building and kicked up snow making it virtually impossible to see beyond a few feet.

"Weather reports coming in are saying it's going to get worse."

"Worse?" Solomon asked.

"Look, I just thought I would give you the heads-up."

"But not all of my guys are in yet."

"Sorry. If the weather changes, we'll call back but we're

shutting down for now."

"And the tourists?"

"What tourists? It's the winter. If there are any, they'll have to hole up there for the night. It's no different from when we close at night."

"Yeah but at least people are aware. Shoot!" Solomon ran a hand over his head thinking about all the complaints that they'd receive. "Okay, Martin."

"Anyway, you've got the key for any emergencies. Stay safe."

"Will do."

He hung up and Solomon stood there gazing out at the extreme weather that had swept in like a sudden tidal wave. Sure, it had got worse overnight, but he figured it would level out as the morning went on, but by the looks of it, that wasn't going to happen anytime soon. He tucked the phone into his pocket and adjusted his duty belt and headed into the office. "Debbie, who have we got in?"

Debbie had long curly hair and wore an extreme

amount of makeup. She was in her late forties and had been working for the department almost as long as Solomon had. She spun around on her chair and tapped a pen against her lower teeth.

"Scott Black, and Lucas Parker. Why?" she asked.

"Where are they?"

"On patrol."

"Did the others call in?"

"Two did to say that they couldn't get through the tunnel."

He sighed. "Yeah, they have to shut it down."

"But it's only morning."

"It's the weather."

Her brow furrowed. "That might explain why the phone line has been up and down."

He reached for a landline phone and picked it up but there was no dial tone. He tried his cell and it appeared to be working but the bars had dropped.

"What about internet?"

"It's up so far."

"Do me a favor and bring up the Weather Channel and give me an update on what's happening. I'm going to make a call." She nodded and started tapping on the keys in front of her. He headed over and picked up the radio and got in touch with Officer Black.

"Hey Scott, we are going to be short on officers today. How are things looking out there?"

"Terrible, chief. I can barely see a damn thing out here. The wind is brutal and the water in the bay is choppy, splashing over onto the dock."

It wasn't uncommon to experience winds that went from sixty to ninety miles an hour, all year round. Over the course of his career, he'd seen it hit vehicles so hard that windshields shattered and it even tore doors off hinges. It certainly wasn't something anyone wanted to be caught out in.

"Listen, Scott, they are shutting the tunnel. I want you and Lucas to head to the Whittier Inn and the Anchor Inn, as well as the harbor, and update folks. I don't want anyone outside. The last thing we need is to deal with a missing person."

In years gone by, there had been those who had wandered and got lost and were never found again. The winters could be brutal and that was without a storm.

"Roger that. And after?" Scott asked.

"Head back here."

"Chief. I saw you with a new guy today, is that the replacement for Danny?"

"Sure is."

"How is he?"

"Seems like a nice enough guy. Time will tell."

The call ended. He slipped into a thick insulated down jacket, poured a coffee and spent the next ten minutes going throughout the building bringing everyone up to speed on the tunnel closure. Most took it well barring a few hotheads who said they had appointments in Anchorage. But that was the cost of working in Whittier. While extreme weather did occur, they usually knew what was coming down the line at least a week out. This had come out of the blue.

It was rare for them to encounter trouble in Whittier. If anything was going to happen it usually occurred in the summer season when tourists overran the town before and after cruises. Still it didn't mean they wouldn't be called upon if the weather knocked out power. It had happened a few years back but thankfully the power company was able to get it up and running within a matter of twenty to thirty minutes.

After doing the rounds and making sure everyone was aware of the situation, he returned to his office and pulled out the file on Alex Riley. He felt bad about calling him in on such short notice, especially since he'd just arrived and wasn't down to start until Monday, but there was no better way to learn the ropes than to be thrown in at the deep end, and besides there was a good chance they wouldn't need to respond to any calls but at least if there were four of them they could cover more ground.

He held up his phone trying to get a signal but all the bars were now gone.

"Great."

"The internet is down as well," Debbie said.

"Let's hope the radios keep working," he said wandering around the office holding his cell high. "I'm going out to see if I can get something."

Solomon wrestled with the front door as if some invisible force was pushing against it. He squeezed out and gasped as high winds pushed him across the icy parking lot. He lifted up his phone and cursed under his breath. "Come on!"

Finally he got two bars.

He dialed in the number for Alex and waited as it rang.

"Hello?" Alex said, his voice crackled over the line. Solomon hoped the connection didn't drop.

"Alex. Ed here. I hate to do this to you, bud, but it looks like I'm going to need you in earlier than Monday."

"No worries. When?"

"Now."

"Now?"

"Yeah, unfortunately the tunnel has been closed and

won't open until tomorrow, and some of the guys who commute can't get in, so we need as many hands on deck as possible. Listen, I know it's last minute but…"

"I'm coming. No problem."

"Right. Thanks."

He already liked his attitude. That was the kind of person they needed in the department; someone who was willing to step up to the plate at a moment's notice. While they had six good officers, not all of them were as willing to come in when one of them was ill. He couldn't blame them, Whittier didn't exactly offer them a thrill ride. He knew that for most of them it was just a stepping-stone to landing a better job in Anchorage. Hell, it wasn't like they paid them much here. It was almost the same as what they got paid while they were going through training but that's because the workload wasn't as heavy.

He hung up and Solomon hit the button on his key fob and hopped into his SUV to collect some paperwork.

* * *

"Who was that?" Jess asked as she started unpacking

clothes and putting them away in the closet.

Alex fished through his bags looking for the uniform they'd given him. "Jess, you seen my uniform?"

"It's in the red suitcase. Why?"

"I have to go in early. Seems the tunnel is closed due to bad weather, and they need an extra hand."

"But we've just arrived. We still have to unpack. I was hoping…"

Alex grabbed up his uniform and came around. "It's fine."

She jerked his head towards the kitchen where Kip was banging around underneath the sink. "And what about him? You going to leave us alone?"

"He's harmless. A little eccentric but harmless."

She groaned with an armful of clothes.

"Jess. This is my job. This is what I signed up for."

"I know, I just…"

"Look, we discussed this. You know about you staying home and all."

"But is it always going to be like this? You darting off

whenever they call?"

He sighed and looked out the window. "The weather is really bad out there. I don't think he would have called me unless it was necessary. Sorry, but I have to go. Okay? If things are fine later, I'll check back in with you but..." He went to give her a kiss on the lips and she turned her cheek. If he had more time, he might have got into it with her but duty called and first impressions mattered. Alex headed out into the kitchen. "Kip, how we doing?"

"Nearly done here. Seems one of the washers needed to be replaced."

"Look, I have to head into work."

"Already?" he asked poking his head out from underneath the sink.

"Afraid so, the tunnel is closed because of the weather and they're short on staff."

Kip glanced at Hayley who had been sitting on the sofa watching him work. "Well you leave this with me."

"Alright. Thanks again."

"No problem."

As he went to head into the bathroom to change, Kip noticed the tattoo on his arm.

"A fellow jarhead. How long you serve?" he asked.

"I did three combat tours. You?"

"Twenty-two years." Kip banged around beneath the sink while looking at him as he got changed with the door open. "So you decided to switch career paths?" he asked.

"Something like that."

Kip nodded.

"You miss it?" Alex asked cutting him a glance as he slipped into a dark navy blue shirt, which went over a white undershirt.

"The work not so much but the brotherhood I do."

"Yeah, that's probably why I opted for the police. That and I needed the job." He started doing up the buttons and came out to tell Hayley to give her mother a hand.

Hayley lowered her cell. "But…"

"No buts. Go."

She groaned and padded into the bedroom.

"Kids," Kip said smiling.

"You got any?" Alex asked.

"One daughter."

"How old?"

"Couldn't tell yah exactly."

"Where's she live?"

"Couldn't tell yah."

Alex raised an eyebrow. "Ah, like that, is it?"

He nodded. "I met her mother when she passed through Whittier about twenty years ago. She was on a cruise. We hit it off, drank a bit too much and well one thing led to another and…" he trailed off. "Anyway, I get this envelope in the mail six months later to say she had gotten pregnant. She told me she didn't want anything from me and neither did she want me to be in the kid's life but she wanted me to know it was a girl and she'd called her Milly."

"And?"

"And that's it. I never heard from her again."

"Man, I'm sorry, that's gotta suck."

"I guess. You don't miss what you never had, right?"

"I know but damn. That's harsh." Alex finished doing up his shirt buttons and started to put on his tie. "Why go to all the trouble of telling you that if she didn't want you to be involved in her life?"

"She figured my life was too complicated. That or she thought I drank too much."

He nodded but decided not to question him on that. It wasn't like he was any better. After the loss of his son, he'd dealt with the grief at the bottom of a bottle. It didn't last long though, eventually he had to step up to the plate when he saw Jess spiraling down. If he hadn't quit, there was no telling what might have happened.

Kip continued, "Truth is, I wasn't drinking much back then. She just caught me on a bad night."

"I've had a few of those."

"I'm sure you have," he said before turning his attention to the faucet. Alex slipped into his ballistic vest that had the word POLICE emblazoned across the front in white.

"Feels good, don't it?"

"What?"

"To feel useful," Kip said.

"Damn right it does."

Kip chuckled. "Well don't expect much action around here, at least not at the level you were operating at."

Alex smiled and stepped back into the bathroom. "Kip. You mind telling me what happened across the way? In apartment 1002?"

He stopped wrenching on the pipe and rose to his feet. An eyebrow rose. "They didn't tell you about that?"

"About?"

He nodded and pursed his lips before trying the faucet. It kicked out more murky water but it soon changed. "The position you're taking is to replace an officer who committed suicide."

"In that room?"

"No. That belonged to his closest friend. Apparently, and I'm only going by rumors swirling in this town, Greg Mitchell, the occupant, had some grow operation going on, there was even talk about heroin and whatnot.

Anyway, there was some big shootout and Greg was killed. Seems Danny couldn't live with the guilt and shot himself at the station, same day."

"Shit."

"Yep, but that's not the worst of it. Danny Lee, the officer that took his life, was extremely close to Solomon. Guy treated him like his own son. Broke the guy's heart after his death. Don't say anything but he hasn't been the same since. I mean people think I drink a lot but that's nothing compared to Solomon. He's often the last one out of the Anchor Inn at night and the last two weekends he hasn't made it back into town. Some say he's starting to lose it. I just notch it up to grief. Danny was a good man. You have big shoes to fill."

"Great. Now I feel the pressure."

Kip laughed and turned off the faucet. "Right. That's that. The light I'll check in a minute. Where's this other leak?"

"In the bedroom. I'll show you."

Kip carried his tools and Alex led him in, and pointed

to the corner of the room.

"That's odd."

"What is?" Alex asked.

"Well…" Kip stepped back out of the room and looked up as if he was following something. "The pipes for each of the apartments run along this wall. If there was a leaky pipe, you would probably see it on this side of the room."

"Maybe someone spilled something on the floor above," Jess said.

"Possible. Anyway, I'll take a look." He crossed the room and pulled up a chair and took out a flashlight and pushed up on the ceiling tile. "Holy cow that's heavy." He gave it a hard shift and then shone his light into the dark, cramped space between the ceiling and the next floor. "Well what the hell have we got here?" He fumbled with the flashlight and then asked Alex to hold on to it. "That's it, give me a bit more light up here."

Kip slid back the tile and yanked on some green material and a huge duffel bag dropped down into his arms. On one end of it was a large wet patch as if a drink had leaked inside of it. He hopped off the chair and crouched down to open the zipper. As soon as he pulled it back, Alex's eyes widened.

Chapter 7

The bitch had seen too much. Had she kept her nose out of their business she might have survived. Leon dragged the owner across the kitchen floor. A week earlier she'd given him this big spiel over the phone about how she'd taken over the place and rebranded it as a health and wellness retreat. Leon had called to book a room on the fifteenth floor, in what was originally called June's Condo Suites, in the hopes of finding the heroin. It was worth over sixty million on the black market, and most of it was already accounted for, that's why it couldn't be overlooked. Leon, Pat and Jimmy had come down a few days earlier to see what they could find out. While they'd never been in Greg Mitchell's apartment until one day ago, they knew him well. He'd been one of their most trusted dealers on the streets of Anchorage before moving back to Whittier to take care of an ailing father. That was ten years ago. That move had presented ideas, one of which was thought up by Greg himself.

"Give me a hand, will yah?" he said to Pat who was smoking a joint as Leon removed the lampstand's power cord from around Theresa's throat. She'd shown up banging on the door early that morning because Pat had ordered in two escorts the night before and someone must have squealed. He recalled the conversation with her only hours earlier.

"I don't run that kind of establishment. Now I want all of you out of here."

"Listen, lady, you must have us mistaken for some other guys as we didn't order in anyone. It's just us. We're down here to hike and fish, that's it."

The frail-looking woman wagged her finger in his face with no idea of who she was dealing with. Behind the door, Pat and Jimmy were smirking, making gestures about cutting her throat. But that wasn't his way. Unlike the others he preferred to use violence as a last resort. It wasn't that he didn't enjoy squeezing the life out of someone or putting a bullet through their skull — hell, he'd done it enough to people and not missed a wink of sleep, however under the circumstances they had to use a bit more tact. Unfortunately she wouldn't listen. Problem was she'd forced her way inside wanting to search the place. Now the hookers had already left two hours before that so there was no fear of her finding them but it wasn't them that caused her death, it was the Beretta on the kitchen table. She nearly had a coronary when she spotted it.

Before she could get a word out, Leon blindsided her with a fist to the head and then used the cord from one of the lampstands to strangle her to death. He couldn't have her rushing out and bringing the cops down on them. Cayden was clear that they weren't to leave until they found his drugs.

"Tough old broad," Pat said. "She didn't go quickly."

"Just give me a hand," he said. He dragged her lifeless body into the middle of the living room and then pulled a knife and cut the carpet around her so he could roll her up. They would take her out back once it was dark and dump her body and let the bears handle the rest. After they would search her records for their booking and get rid of any trace of them being there. It wasn't like it was the first time they'd killed.

"You should have seen her face when she laid eyes on that gun. I thought she was going to shit herself," Jimmy added. Pat laughed.

Pat and Jimmy were brothers. Pat was the older of the two, he towered over Jimmy, a gangly sonofabitch with more legs than upper body. Jimmy was the complete opposite, short, pure muscle. Leon would wind them up and say they came from two different mothers as the resemblance just wasn't there. Leon on the other hand was square faced, flat nosed with round eyes and wavy hair. His nose had been busted up from one too many scraps as a kid and had never fully set right, so it was slightly off to the side. Those who poked fun at him while he was growing up had been quickly dealt with. He was the scrapper of the bunch, someone who enjoyed getting his knuckles bloody and being hands-on when it came to killing a person. Pat liked his knives, and Jimmy didn't care how he killed, but those who died by his hand were unrecognizable when it was over.

Jimmy stood by the window looking out through binoculars that were left on the windowsill by the owner for whale watching. "You think Cayden will get here? What with the weather and all?"

"If he says he's coming he'll be here," Leon said.

They rolled the woman like a pita, turning her over until she disappeared inside the drab-looking carpet. Once it was done they stepped back and stared down at their handiwork. Pat handed Leon a half-smoked joint and he took a hard pull and exhaled a cloud.

The lights flickered above, and Leon looked up. He groaned. This was the last place he wanted to be because he'd told his gal he was planning on taking her away, somewhere warm. At the last minute Cayden called and asked him to do a run. He'd argued back and forth that the chances of finding the drugs were slim to none — more than likely the cops had them in storage — but

Cayden seemed unfazed. That was just like him. It didn't matter what obstacle was in his path, Cayden didn't see it. Perhaps that was why he'd stuck with him so long. They'd known each other from their days in school. Even as far back as then they'd dabbled in the illegal, mostly petty crime, breaking into vehicles and factories in Anchorage, all low-key stuff but it had given them a taste for it. Cayden had been driven by the thrill of the hunt. It was like a drug to him, and in some ways if he was honest, Leon enjoyed it too. Both of them had dropped out of school, never got their GED but they didn't care because by the age of seventeen they were stealing cars and selling them privately on the black market and pocketing the lion's share. Sitting in a chair across from the dead woman, taking turns toking on the joint, he thought back to those days, how simple and easy it all was. There was no bloodshed, no territory issues, the insurance companies covered the loss of vehicles for the original owners and they were turning a tidy profit. But that was twenty years ago, long before Cayden had made connections, and aspired to make a name. Now their hands were covered in blood, their consciences scarred and they were forever looking over their shoulder. It wasn't just the police they had to worry about but guys like them — those looking to make a name for themselves. They weren't getting any younger, and it was only a matter of time before their luck ran out. The question of who would end their string of luck was still to be answered.

Jimmy turned towards Leon as they sat there waiting for Cayden to show.

"I still don't get it. I mean you told him we couldn't find it. What does he hope to achieve coming all the way down here?" he asked.

Leon was still lost in thought when Pat replied.

"All I know is some people are going to die," he said reaching for a bottle of beer and knocking it back. He jabbed his finger at Jimmy. "And when he does show up. Keep your trap shut. I don't want you putting your foot in your mouth like you did back in July."

"What? I was just being honest."

"Yeah and that honesty is liable to get you killed, brother."

"Please. You act like you're afraid of him."

"You should be," Leon said without taking his eyes off the roll of carpet in front of him. He then looked at Jimmy. "You want to stay above ground, I would strongly advise you to heed the word of your brother."

"Fair enough. But tell me this, Leon. You've known Cayden longer than any of us. Why do you stick around?"

Leon reached into his pocket and pulled out a photo of his wife and baby. It was an honest question, and one that both he and his lady had asked many a time. He wasn't sure why, maybe it was loyalty, greed, or plain stupidity but Cayden had been there for him through his rough upbringing, he'd been there on the nights his old man had beaten him so hard he couldn't walk. No matter how he looked at it, they were in this for life or at least until he could talk Cayden into walking away from it.

There was a thump at the door, four times and all

three of them jumped up and pulled their handguns. Leon put his hand out to tell the others not to move as he made his way over and peered through the peephole. He smiled and unlocked the door, then pulled it open.

"Cayden."

Cayden smiled. "Hello boys."

He entered with six more men, Vic, Hank, Ty, Raymond, Chris and Jerome. It was rare they all showed up unless something serious was about to happen. Leon closed the door behind them and Cayden walked into the center of the room and looked down at the roll of carpet. He cast a glance at Leon.

"It was necessary," Leon said.

He smiled. "I didn't say it wasn't. Now, you going to pour me a drink? As it was a hell of a ride getting here."

Pat hurried over to the kitchen and returned with bottles of beer, and bourbon and passed them around. Cayden was wearing a long black leather trench coat and a black beanie hat that was covered in snow. He shook it off but didn't take a seat which made it clear that he wasn't there to waste time.

"So which room was Greg in?"

"1002," Leon replied.

"And you tore the place apart?"

"Pretty much," Jimmy replied.

Leon knew Cayden didn't like Jimmy. They'd already been in talks about whether they thought he should be knocked off but Pat had gone to bat for him and promised to keep him in line. It wasn't that he wasn't good at his job, he just wasn't the kind of yes-man that Cayden like to have around him. He questioned too much, and Cayden didn't like having to explain or justify his actions. Cayden scowled at Jimmy.

Pat cleared his throat. "Yeah, we did. Tore up the furniture, anywhere it could have been stored we opened, looked under, above. You name it, we've done it, boss."

Cayden sucked air between his teeth and looked around like he was disgusted. "And yet I still have no drugs before me, so here's what we're going to do. There is a room on the fifteenth floor just down the corridor."

"The homeowners lounge, yeah, we saw it."

"Right, well, we are going to get everyone in it."

"Boss?" Pat asked.

"You heard me. I want you to start down on the ground floor, going door to door, force them, drag them out, hell, shoot them if they won't go but I want everyone in that room. I think it shouldn't take too long to figure out where those drugs are stored. I know they're here because our guy who brought them confirmed it, as did Greg and that pig before his untimely demise. Your job is to find them."

"And what are you going to do?" Jimmy asked.

Pat piped up. "Shut up, Jimmy."

"No. No. He wants to know," Cayden said walking over to him. "I'm going to be keeping a close eye on the group and dealing with the cops. Any other questions?"

He shook his head and Cayden continued, "Greg was a fucking idiot. I think we can all agree on that. The only reason I kept him around was because he hadn't screwed up. I knew eventually he would, I just didn't anticipate it being on the largest haul we've had since we got this operation up and running. But, what can you do? Now having been the one to collect in those early days, I know he kept the drugs in his apartment. He didn't leave them outside because of the temperatures and he sure as hell didn't ask someone else to look after the drugs. However, that's not to say that he didn't change things up. Danny, the pig, told us that he stored them in a safe place in this building. So either the drugs are with the police or they're in this building somewhere."

"But, boss, this is a big place," Pat said.

"And that was a big fucking shipment. I want it found. It will be found if I have to kill every fucking person in this shit hole to find it." He breathed in deeply and looked at Leon. "And that includes the police," he said before taking another swig of bourbon and walking over to the window to look out.

Leon knew he wasn't joking. He'd seen that look in his eyes many times over the past two years. He was back to using, probably coked up. He'd told him to get clean because it only screwed with his mind but trying to talk sense into him was pointless. The last time he'd tried to have the conversation he'd blown his top and threatened Leon. The fact was Cayden had changed, the power had gone to his head, the drugs only made it worse and the friend he once knew was hidden below layers of hate, greed and narcissism. That's why he'd wanted to get away with his lady — to think over his involvement, and to seriously consider walking away from it all. Now he wished he had.

"About the cops," Leon said. "I'm with you on this but if we open fire, start dragging people out, we are going to bring SWAT down on us faster than a New York minute." It was his last attempt at trying to get him to think of the consequences. Without turning, Cayden lifted his cell phone.

"No one's coming. There is no signal, and the tunnel is closed."

"Closed?"

"Yeah, we were lucky to get in. Soon as we were on the

other side they brought it down. Something to do with the weather, a cop said. Oh, and about those cops. There are only three of them on duty. No SWAT are showing up here and we'll be long gone by the time they do."

Awkward silence fell over them for a few seconds before Cayden yelled, "Well what are you waiting for? Get on with it!"

Vic dumped a bag on the ground, unzipped it and starting handing out M4 carbines.

Chapter 8

The entire bag was stuffed with bricks of heroin or cocaine, it was hard to tell by all the wrapping but it was definitely drugs. Alex fished out brick after brick and placed it on the bed until he saw what had caused the leak. In the bottom corner was a half-filled plastic bottle of juice. The top wasn't sealed tight and so most of it had leaked out, soaked through the bag and stained the ceiling tile.

"What the hell…?" Hayley said.

"Hayley, go into the living room," Jess said.

She didn't protest and left immediately. All three of them stood there staring at it.

"Kip, the room across the way. The tape over the door was snapped. Did you do that or one of the officers?" Alex asked.

"I noticed that on the way in, I was going to check after."

"So it happened recently?"

"Well it wasn't like that a couple of days ago because I was up here fixing someone's plumbing."

He nodded. "Okay, listen, I'll get this over to the department," Alex said tossing it all back into the bag haphazardly. "Maybe Solomon will know more about it."

The light in the room started to flicker then it went out.

Kip crossed the room and flipped the switch a couple of times. He tried a few more rooms before returning. "Great. I'll have to check the fuse box. Must be the storm."

Outside the wind had picked up and was howling. Although it was still daytime, it was hard to tell as it was so blustery and overcast it felt like early evening. Dark storm clouds had moved in squeezing out whatever light remained. Alex hauled the strap over his shoulder, and cast a glance at his phone. There were no bars. "Damn it."

"It's out?" Kip asked.

"Appears so." He went and collected his firearm that was locked inside a gun case, and palmed a magazine into it. He put two more in his duty belt, holstered his service weapon and headed for the door.

"You got a landline?" Kip asked.

"The phone is in one of the boxes," Alex said.

"Forget it, I'll check the one downstairs."

"Alex," Jess called out. "What if the power doesn't come back on?"

"We have two backup gasoline generators downstairs," Kip said. "They need to be fired up but it should provide enough power while we try to figure out what the issue is."

"It has enough power for the entire building?"

"Of course. After some of the ice storms we've had over the years we had to get it. Quite a few of our residents are senior citizens. They can't be climbing the stairwells in an emergency. The backup generators can provide enough power to cook, have lights, stay warm and potentially keep us in contact with the outside world.

That is if the internet hasn't gone down." He looked around. "You guys got any flashlights?"

"My service one," Alex said raising his.

Jessica looked flustered. "And I think we have another one somewhere around here. Finding it is another thing. The rest of our belongings weren't meant to arrive until tomorrow."

"Like furniture?" Kip asked.

"We couldn't bring all of it but we have a truck that's bringing some down from Anchorage," Alex said. He opened the door to the hallway. Outside it was really dark because there were no windows. He pulled out the Maglite he'd been issued for work and switched it on, shining it on the door across the way. He reached for the door handle and noticed that it wasn't locked. The door was slightly ajar. Alex entered apartment 1002 and shone his light. It washed over the silhouette of furniture. Kip came up behind him, using his own flashlight.

"Dear lord. Doug is going to have a fit when he sees this mess. Who the hell did this?"

They entered to find that all the furniture had been torn apart. Chunks of sofa filling was scattered. Tables were flipped and cupboards yanked off their hinges. Alex went into the bedroom and found the mattress ripped down the middle as if someone had gone wild with a knife.

"You said Greg Mitchell lived here, right?"

"Yeah."

"And he was dealing?" Alex asked.

"Well I can speculate on that but rumor has it he was running a grow op."

"You think he was dealing in heroin?" Alex asked turning to Kip who was looking around the room in total bewilderment. Kip shrugged. "If he was he kept it under wraps. Though that's hard to do in a building like this, where everyone knows each other's business. Sometimes they know too much." He turned and walked out and Alex followed him into the hallway. Some of the residents of the building on the tenth floor had come out of their apartments and were chatting about the blackout. The moment they laid eyes on Kip they started firing questions.

"What's going on?"

"I was in the middle of cooking."

"When is the power coming back on?"

Kip raised both hands to try and calm them. "Please, people. Go back inside your homes. We'll have the power on as soon as we can. The storm has knocked it out."

"Typical. They really need to update the wiring in this place."

"It's not the building, Janice, and they already have. The storm has forced the tunnel to be shut down and you're not the only ones affected. And please don't line up outside the store if the lights aren't on in half an hour. It will probably get worse before it gets better. Now go on back inside. Grab a flashlight, use some candles but just make sure you don't leave them unattended. The last thing I need on my plate is to have to deal with a fire."

Both of them squeezed through unhappy residents as they made their way to the stairwell. "Before you head over to the department, Alex. Do you think you can give me a hand filling up the generators?"

Alex grimaced. "Kip, I really should get moving."

"It'll only take a few minutes. If we can get the power back up that will at least get these folks off my back. By now there is probably a line a mile long outside my store."

Alex frowned and nodded, and they headed into the stairwell and made their way down to the basement. "Kip, you mentioned you had been warning people about a superstorm for the past four years. Why are you so obsessed with it?"

He laughed. "I'm not obsessed. I guess it comes from my time in the military. I just think you need to be prepared. Too many folks are putting their faith in the government and let's face it, they are in the same boat as us. Anyway, there's not a lot to do when I'm working. When I'm not serving the odd customer in the store and believe me we don't get many, I listen to the radio."

"Why?"

"Because old habits die hard."

"No, I meant regarding customers."

"Oh," he said smiling. "That's because of the high prices."

"So lower them."

Kip snorted. "Supply and demand, my friend. Supply and demand! Most of the residents here travel to Anchorage once a month and spend upwards of fifteen hundred bucks at Costco to stock up their cupboards so they don't have to pay me. It's only the lazy or those who forgot an item that usually come into the store. Anyway when I'm not manning the desk I help Doug with the maintenance. Between the two of us we manage to keep this place ticking over."

"Seems like it needs an overhaul."

"Already had one back in 2016. We finally managed to get a three million dollar grant from the U.S. Department of Agriculture to cover repairs, repaint the building and get a decent boiler."

"Boiler?"

"When the military ran this place they had their own

heating plant but when they pulled out they installed two boilers. One of them quit working and so the water in the pipes ended up freezing and we had pipes bursting all over the place. Finally they managed to get rid of those two and replaced the corroded pipes with PVC and installed three modern boilers so we are all good now. However, without power to run them and with the frigid temperatures we are having right now, there is a chance we might find ourselves back at square one." They eventually made it to the basement. "Oh and that's not all, this building and the Buckner one originally had asbestos in the flooring so all of that had to be ripped out and replaced along with an air exchange system and floating walls to cover the cinder block walls in the hallways so it didn't look like a damn institution, and it allows for them to paint it easier."

"You like living here, Kip?"

"Could be worse."

"How?"

He snorted. "Look, on the surface this place might

seem like a junkyard and at times, believe me, I have thought about moving away, especially when you hear fishermen say, 'There is nothing shittier than Whittier,' but I'll tell you this… there is something special to the people in this place. The ones who stay, I mean. You feel like part of a family. That's lost in the big cities. It's the closest thing that I have to the sense of brotherhood I found in the military. When I got out, I tried to keep in touch with pals but like everything eventually people go their separate ways and you have to get on and live. But how do you handle life outside of the times when you're working? You know, when you're not keeping your mind busy?"

They pushed their way through a set of doors in the basement.

"So you wouldn't want to live in Anchorage?" Alex asked.

"What would I do there? Who would I know? At least here I know where I stand. I see the same people, day in and day out, and while it might not seem very fulfilling, I feel useful, and this place feels like one big dorm room."

He chuckled and began pointing out a few rooms in the basement. "You got many belongings arriving tomorrow?"

"A fair amount."

"Well whatever can't be stored in your apartment can be contained in these storage cages. Costs $15 a month though. There is also a room full of chest freezers. People eat a lot of fish here so you might want to get yourself one of those. They are $15 a month. Oh, and the laundry costs $25 a month."

"Twenty-five bucks?"

"That's not bad if you're doing a few loads of washing every other day."

They continued on. "That tunnel over there runs from the building to the school which is on the west side."

"Why did they build that?"

He stifled a laugh. "Management will say it's for convenience and because of the weather but that's bull crap. It's because of the bears."

"Bears?"

"Oh yeah, we get them rooting through the dumpsters outside the trash room on the ground floor. We usually have to bang on the door before heading out as you never know when you're going to come face to face with one of those hairy suckers. We had one wander into the school. Scared the shit out of the pupils."

"Anyone get hurt?"

"Nope."

"How did you get it out?"

"My rifle."

"The one in your store?"

He cast a sideways glance and grinned. "You're in God's country now, Alex. Got to be prepared."

"Speaking of being prepared. How old is this place?" he asked looking around.

"Over sixty years old. But don't let it fool you. It's as strong as an ox. It's survived all manner of storms. On Good Friday back in 1964, it survived the Alaskan quake. This place was still standing. Of course some people died."

"How?"

"The tsunami from the quake. It came in off the bay and hit this building like a wall. Over a hundred feet high. Damn thing killed thirteen people."

"So it's true, the bay doesn't freeze, does it?"

"Nope. Too deep. Had it done, they might have survived."

"So this superstorm. You don't think it would kick up another tsunami, do you?"

He shrugged. "Hard to know. I'm not going to say it won't because I've been monitoring what's been going on over the last four years and it doesn't look good."

"Yeah, that's what that climatologist said. He thinks it would make Superstorm Sandy look like child's play."

"It will. There's a good chance it will throw us back to the ice age."

"You serious?" Alex asked.

They entered a large room that had three boilers inside of it, industrial generators with gasoline canisters. Kip shone his light around the room. The light hit a shelf full of about twenty mason jars, some of them were filled, others empty.

"What are those?"

Kip's eyebrows rose. "Ah, my private stash of moonshine." He walked over and took one down and unscrewed the top, then stuck it under Alex's nose. It smelled like ass. "You want to try some?"

"Thanks, I think I'll give it a pass."

He laughed. "Over there, grab that canister and I'll grab the other. Fill up that generator." They went about doing that and Kip continued talking. "It's all to do with global warming and the melting of the ice caps. Without getting too technical, much of our weather over land is determined by the ocean's rotating currents, which are occurring north and south of the equator. Essentially we have the cold heading south and the warmer waters heading north. Studies show that when that Gulf Stream flow is reduced, it can trigger an ice age kind of like what was seen in northwestern Europe back in the thirteenth to the nineteenth centuries. It caused long winters, shorter growing seasons and increased glaciers. Yep, it's not pretty and the fact is people really don't know how Mother Nature is going to respond. They try to come up with these timelines but she's unpredictable and after all the damage we've done I wouldn't be surprised if she hits back just to remind us of how small we are."

"You know a lot about this."

"Nah, I just listen. The fact is global warming has been causing the ice caps to melt for a long time. That's been sending out large amounts of fresh cold water into the oceans which can disturb the current enough to change the weather on land. Basically, if we keep going the way we are using fossil fuels instead of renewable energy, we are going to take a nosedive into a cold snap that could last for decades or even longer." He stopped filling the generator and placed the canister on the ground. "And you know the irony, other parts of the world will stay warm."

"I'm not sure I understand."

"Okay think of like a conveyer belt. Warm water is lighter than cold water. So you have this current heading up from the Gulf floating on top of the cold water and so it keeps moving. You then have the northern Atlantic cooling it down, making it denser and then it flows back to the south crossing underneath the northern warm Gulf Stream until it hits the tropics and the cycle repeats. But if you get too much dilution in the ocean through the ice caps melting, it will make the water get lighter and essentially choke out and stall the entire system. The sea levels rise, temperatures change and all manner of extreme weather occurs in the atmosphere."

"So what's the solution at that point?"

"There is no solution. We head south." He laughed. "Join the snowbirds and wait for Mother Nature to sort her shit out."

Alex poured in the gasoline from a large canister.

"How much fuel we got?"

"Enough down here for maybe 24 hours."

Once it was filled up Kip fired up the generators and

stood back as they rumbled to life. He looked up at the lights as they flickered to life and illuminated the whole room. “There we go. That should keep them off my doorstep.”

“You just made two hundred people happy, Kip.”

“Two hundred?”

“The residents in the building.”

He scoffed. “There haven’t been two hundred people here since 2015. This place has around a hundred residents, plus or minus twenty depending on the time of the year. Yeah, the turnover is pretty high. Tourists don’t stay for longer than an afternoon usually, and new residents come and go. It’s the isolation. It can get to you.”

“Solomon said. Which reminds me, I should get over there before he comes looking for me. I figure he’ll be interested in this.” Alex heaved the large duffel bag back onto his shoulder. They turned to leave when the echo of rapid gunfire erupted. Both of them froze as the sound of screams filled the air.

Chapter 9

Cayden figured the quickest way to round up the residents was to start on the lower floors. Those higher up had nowhere to go. Two men per floor, ten of them, they were going to clear five floors at a time. What had started out as a pretty straightforward request had already led to the death of one resident causing others to scream in fear. He had no qualms about ending lives. Sixty million dollars in heroin was worth it. First order of business was to lock all the lower exit doors. No one was getting in or out without his permission. Once everyone was out of their apartments and brought to the homeowners lounge on the fifteenth floor, he would take the subtle approach; question them and hope someone would provide answers on where Greg had stashed it.

Cayden was on the fifth floor.

He banged on a door with the back of his rifle. "Let's go. Open up!"

Those who chose not to open were quickly dealt with. He gave them a minute or two to reach the door but if they took any longer than that he opened fire, kicked the door open and threatened to take their lives.

"How we doing, Leon?"

"You know this is a dumb move, Cayden."

If anyone else had said that, they would have been swallowing teeth but he and Leon went far back. Sure, the dynamics between them had changed over the years as he moved into a leading role and Leon assisted, but he still respected him. Sometimes he was right but not this time.

"I gave you plenty of time to find it."

Leon pushed a resident towards the stairwell at the end of the hall. "Head on up to the homeowners lounge, now!" The frightened mother with two children cowered and hurried down the hallway following the long line of people. Most were compliant. Everyone was afraid.

Keeping his M4 low, he grabbed a hold of Cayden and shoved him against the wall. "You know what, Cayden, your need to be in control is wearing my patience thin."

"Then go. You don't have to be here."

Leon released him and returned to pulling residents out of their apartments. Cayden fired a few shots to keep them on their toes, to keep them compliant, to keep them from heroics. Once they cleared the fifth floor, they traipsed up the stairwell. He was pleased to see the power had come back on. For a few minutes there he'd got worried they were going to be faced with an even greater problem. Searching apartments in the dark wouldn't have been easy. It didn't take them long to clear rooms. Most residents were too damn scared to fight back, and those that did were dropped.

Pat and Jimmy shoved the last three people into the lounge. It could comfortably entertain up to 50 guests but it was cramped now. They'd managed to squeeze seventy-two people in there by stacking chairs and folding tables and seating everyone on the floor. It had a small kitchenette and a small bathroom off to the right of the entrance. Two large windows provided a blurry view of the harbor.

Cayden walked out into the middle of the room and the residents parted like the Red Sea, cowering back, clinging to their children, some mumbling curse words under their breath. He looked out the window and cupped a hand to his ear.

"You hear that?" he asked, turning to a room of frightened faces. "That's the sound of help not coming. Get used to it." He breathed in deeply allowing his mind to work through what he wanted to say. "Now listen up. I'm going to make this real easy. Tenth floor, room 1002. Greg Mitchell had something that belonged to me. Unfortunately he can't be here to tell me where it is. That's where you fine folks come in. Who here knows anything about what happened the day he died?"

His eyes surveyed the faces as he walked among them. "Come on now. This can all be over real soon if you just speak up. No harm will come to you."

"Then why did you kill my husband?" a woman yelled, clutching her two kids. He turned fast on the balls of his feet.

"Your husband was given clear directions. He refused to follow them. Let me make something clear. If I ask you a question, you answer it. If I tell you to move, you move. Any deviation from this will have dire consequences. Do I make myself clear?"

No one responded, so he lifted his gun and pointed at the lady. "Do I make myself clear?"

"Yes. Yes." All over the room people replied.

"Very good. Now we understand each other, let's move this along, shall we? Who knows what happened the day he died?"

"I do," a kid in his late teens replied.

"Tommy, enough," his mother said.

Cayden smiled. "No. It's okay, Tommy. Come on up here."

He hesitated for a second but then rose to his feet and worked his way through the crowd coming to a stop a few feet from Cayden. "Well?"

The kid was a stringy-looking fellow, blond hair down to his jawline. He was wearing a thick green school sweater with the words Whittier Eagles on the front, stone-washed jeans and a pair of worn Nikes. He stuck his hands into his pockets and spoke with his head down like he was afraid to look Cayden in the eyes. "It was a drug bust."

"Okay. And?"

"He was killed by the police for growing pot."

"And you know this because?"

"I saw them hauling twenty plants out of there."

"Seems like overkill," Cayden said.

"It wasn't just that. I overheard one of the cops being accused of trafficking heroin."

"Tommy?"

Tommy turned towards his mother.

"It's true. I told Officer Lee that Greg sold me weed, and without him knowing followed him to the apartment. I heard it all."

Cayden nodded, walked over and put his arm around Tommy, causing his mother to look worried. "Don't worry, mom, I won't touch one hair." He turned back to

Tommy. "So did you see them haul out the heroin?"

"Well no, that's the thing. Officer Lee denied it, but Chief Solomon must have believed it because he pulled me into the station two days after Danny took his life to ask me questions about whether Greg had offered me heroin."

"And did he?"

"No, it was just pot." He looked back at his mother. "I swear."

"So you have no idea where he stashed this heroin?"

"That's why you're here, isn't it?" an older gentleman piped up. Cayden turned to face him.

"You know something, old man?"

He shook his head, giving Cayden a defiant look. "No."

"Then shut your mouth." He looked back at Tommy. "Tommy, did you ever visit his apartment? See where he went in town?"

"He rarely left the building," a woman across the room said.

"And you are?" Cayden asked.

"Clara Timmins. Teacher. Besides heading to Anchorage once a month he stayed in his apartment. My apartment is on the same floor, apartment 1005."

"Ah, a teacher. And so did you ever see him wandering the corridors, maybe taking a smoke outside? Out of his room at unusual hours?"

"I might know my neighbors but I'm not intrusive. They have a right to privacy, as do I." She had her arm around a young teen boy, with dark hair buzzed at the sides and long on top.

"Is that your boy?" Cayden asked showing interest in him.

"No, he's a student of mine."

"What's your name, boy?"

He pursed his lips tight refusing to speak.

"His name is Ben."

"The cat got your tongue, Ben?"

"He's autistic, asshole."

"Doesn't mean he can't answer."

"You're scaring him."

Ben looked down at the M4 in his hand.

"Why don't you leave the kids alone?" a woman said across the room.

Cayden scoffed. "And you are?"

"Jess Riley."

"Well Jess. While adults tend to have the attention span of a gnat, children tend to see more than we give them credit. Now I saw all the kids running up and down these halls. I know they spend a great deal of time going from apartment to apartment. And having been a kid myself I know where they go when they want to get away from restrictive, overbearing parents. So let me do the questioning, okay?"

He waited for a response but she never gave it. She was a fine-looking woman, certainly the best out of those in the room. She had a small face and all her features were well proportioned, a tight body and dark wavy hair that was pulled back in a pony. He glanced at the teen girl beside her.

"What have you seen?" he asked her.

The woman wrapped her arms around her kid. "I told you, leave the kids alone."

Cayden cocked his head catching the defiance in her tone. He worked his way across the room and stood in front of her, sweeping his rifle behind his back. He reached up and took a hold of her face and squished it, causing her mouth to open ever so slightly. He was tempted to kiss her but instead he stared into her eyes then flicked his hand away causing her head to jerk to one side.

"What's your name?" he asked the daughter.

"Hayley."

"She doesn't know anything. She's new," the same old man who had spoken earlier said.

"New?" He laughed. "Lady, I have got to hear the reason you came to this shit hole."

She didn't respond.

"So when did you arrive?"

"Today."

"Her husband's a cop," someone in the crowd said.

He frowned and looked back at her. "Is that true?"

She didn't say a word, so he grabbed her by the face again. "Lady, you are really pushing my buttons."

"It is," she said.

"And what's his name?"

"Does it matter?"

He chuckled. "Just tell me his name."

She was hesitant and he picked up on that. In all his years dealing with the police he had run across all types, those looking to make money on the side, those looking to take him down and those who had something to hide.

"Name!" Cayden bellowed.

"Alex."

"And where would Alex be?"

"Working."

"Huh?" He breathed in deeply. "Dead cop. New cop. Interesting." He rolled his lower lip under his top teeth and motioned to Vic with his head. "Keep a close eye on this one."

Cayden walked away thinking there was no point in questioning someone who had just arrived. He returned to Tommy, looked at him then put the question out to everyone in the room. "Well if no one is going to speak up, we'll have to tear apart your apartments because I know damn well someone isn't telling me the truth here."

He turned to Hank. "Take some of the men, start on floor ten and go through every apartment, tear them apart."

"You can't do that," a man said rising to his feet.

Pat was quick to respond by slamming the butt of his rifle into the guy's face, making him drop to his knees. "Stay the fuck down."

Cayden walked over to the man who was groping a bloodied face and he crouched down in front of him. "We'll do whatever the hell we like."

The man spit blood in his face and cursed at him. A pin hitting the floor could have been heard. Cayden slowly pulled a handkerchief from his pocket and wiped the blood away. As he placed it back in his pocket, his slipped his fingers in the brass knuckles, squeezed tight and in one smooth move fired a right hook at the man's jaw. He tumbled back and Cayden was on him like a lion, throwing punch after punch at his face until he was unrecognizable and no longer breathing. Women and children screamed even as his men tried to get them to be quiet. Once Cayden was done, he rose to his feet and glanced at the people. Sometimes the only way to keep people in line was to give a demonstration. It was how he'd done it years ago when he was trying to establish his business in Anchorage. People understood fear.

Staring at the horrified room full of parents blocking their children's eyes, he asked, "Questions?"

No one said a word as Hank and five others left the room in search of the drugs.

* * *

Across the room Jess sat in silence, Hayley sobbing on her chest. Outside the weather was getting worse, the wind was howling and heavy snow blanketed the town. Her eyes flitted to the dead body of the man that had been left there as a warning to others. She'd never seen anyone murdered. She felt sick and nauseated in the pit of her stomach. Hearing his bones break, seeing that kind of brutality made every fiber of her being nervous. She clung to Hayley and whispered into her ear.

"It's okay, hon, it's okay. Dad will get help. He'll come."

Hayley looked up at her with unconvinced eyes.

Her mind flashed back to years earlier, the night they lost their son Ethan. Learning to live with Alex away from home was hard but when their second child came along and she was suffering from postpartum depression, she barely could hold it together. When Ethan came down with what she assumed was a normal case of the flu, she did what any mother would do and got it treated. Even after they saw a doctor and he was given a steroid treatment, she assumed things were okay. A few days passed and he started complaining that he wasn't feeling well, started throwing up and was hit with a high fever. She rushed him to the hospital and within an hour he was critically ill. The medical team did everything they could to save him but he died within three hours.

Even though she'd contacted Alex, he wasn't able to get back in time.

Overcome by grief, she broke down in the hallway of Anchorage Regional Hospital, unable to console Hayley. She'd never felt so alone or lost as in that moment. Now once again she was back there, dealing with a threat to the life of her child.

She trusted Alex.

She believed he would do everything in his power to help but she wasn't going to rely on him. If she'd learned anything through the loss of her son, it was that she would do anything to protect Hayley. She glanced up at the man others were calling Cayden with a look of disdain. She eyed the doorway and her mind started to formulate a plan of escape.

Chapter 10

Alex stood in the west stairwell on the first floor watching the armed intruders go from one apartment to the next. They cursed loudly and tossed items out into the hallway. The sound of glass breaking, material being torn and furniture being destroyed dominated. Kip stood nearby trying to peer around his arm.

"What's going on?" he asked quietly.

He'd cracked the door just slightly, just enough to get a good look at the situation. After hearing the screams they'd quickly made their way up just in time to witness them shoving people towards the east stairwell. They'd heard them ordering residents up to the homeowners lounge. Alex's heart was pounding in his chest. By the time he made it up to the tenth floor his apartment was empty. He saw Hayley's iPhone laying on the kitchen floor, the screen cracked. His mind was churning over, trying to make sense of what was going on. He now had his answers.

In the stairwell he pulled Kip towards the stairs.

"They're looking for this," he said patting the duffel bag. "We need to get Solomon."

He nodded and they hurried back down into the basement, then raced through the long underground tunnel that would take them over to the school in hopes of exiting there. As soon as they came around the corner that led down to the double doors their hearts sank. Wrapped around the metal door handles were thick chains and a large padlock. Alex shook it and shoved against the door but it was wrapped too tight.

He pulled his firearm to shoot the lock but Kip placed his hand on it. "No. They'll hear."

"And?"

"We need to stay low-key."

"Shit!" Alex paced trying to think. "Any other way out?"

"No, other than here, the front has two entrances, and the rear leads out to the dumpsters but they've probably locked those and have men watching the entrances."

"What about the windows on the first floor?"

"With the glass-shattering winds we get in this town, you aren't going to be able to smash one of those, at least not without some difficulty. They were all reinforced after the last storm we had."

"I meant to climb out," he said.

Kip snorted. "Perhaps, if you can enter an apartment without being spotted. You saw how many armed men were out there."

"So we draw them away."

Kip shook his head. "We don't know how many there are. No. It's not worth it." He pointed to the bag. "If they want this, just give it to them. They'll leave and maybe, just maybe no more people will die."

Alex ran a hand over his head. "Are you serious? You can't be that naïve, can you? The residents have seen their faces. If they would shoot people for not doing what they say, do you really think they are going to let all those witnesses live?" Alex leaned into him. "Right now, the only bargaining chip we have is this bag. We hand that over, everyone is as good as dead."

He went over to the wall and took a fire extinguisher off a hook and smashed it against the thick glass multiple times. It cracked but not completely. He tried again, taking his frustration out, but the crack didn't get any wider.

"I told you they reinforced the windows. With the bears wandering, and heavy winds, it costs too much to replace windows."

Alex cursed and tossed the fire extinguisher on the ground. All he could think about was Jess and Hayley. He pulled out his cell to check for a signal. There was still nothing. Kip walked over and put a hand on his shoulder.

"Listen. There is a landline phone in my store. If we can reach it, we might be able to call over to the department. The landlines draw their power from the telephone company. The lines are buried. The phone company usually has a backup generator in place as well."

"Right." He nodded, and they headed for the first

floor. As they got closer to the stairwell, they heard voices.

"You want us to check the basement?"

"Yeah. Take Jerome with you," a male replied.

Alex and Kip backed up fast, hurrying down towards the storage area. Kip led the way. "Follow me."

They darted into a large unfinished room full of storage cages. It was like a huge gym locker with chain-link fencing. The cages were jam-packed with belongings, items that couldn't fit in people's apartments. Alex surveyed the area looking for anywhere to hide. There was nowhere unless they locked themselves in one of the white freezers but that would no doubt be checked. The freezers took up most of the space in the concrete room. There were pallets pushed up against the wall, along with taller freezers spread out. At the far end was another storage area behind a chain-link fence. Kip darted towards it and began fumbling with a set of keys he fished out of his pocket. "Come on. Come on," he muttered.

The sound of voices was getting closer.

Finally he inserted a key and twisted the lock and they

entered.

"Here, help me push this out of the way." Behind the cage were multiple cupboards around six feet in height, old washing machines and all manner of crap. Kip got behind one cupboard and started shifting it, and Alex gave him a hand, putting his shoulder into it. They moved it enough to squeeze behind, then did their best to remain hidden. Both men crouched and waited in the silence. Alex gripped the Glock in his hand, ready to attack if need be.

"I'm telling you we are wasting our time," a man's voice said. Alex shifted position and tried to peer through a gap between two cupboards. He saw an African American male enter the room along with another guy who was white. "Ah, you know Greg. The guy was an asshole. I bet you a dime to a dollar he faked his death and took off with those drugs. He's probably living it up somewhere on some tropical island while we're here freezing our asses off and risking our necks."

"He wouldn't do that."

"No?"

"The guy was a coward. He says he left because of his old man but that's a lie. He left Anchorage because he thought Cayden was going to kill him because of a few deals that went bad. The fact was if it weren't for me, he would have been dead a long time ago. I covered for his ass multiple times. I wouldn't be surprised if someone got to him. You know, that cop or one of the dealers he burned back in Anchorage."

Alex watched them lifting up the doors on the freezers and peering inside.

"Still, do you honestly think he would be dumb enough to keep the drugs in this building? I think we should be looking at that cop's place in Girdwood. My money is that he carried them out and stashed them, then Greg bumped him off and made it look like suicide."

The guy laughed. "You talk too much. Now start looking."

They went one by one through each of the freezers, lifting them up and tossing out large amounts of frozen fish and meat onto the ground. "This is a joke! Do you see Cayden doing any of this?"

"Just get on with it," the black guy said.

"He's gone over the edge. Don't you think?"

"I think if you keep whining he's going to throw you over an edge. Probably off the top of this building. Now keep your mouth shut and do what he's paying you to do."

The white guy laughed. "You really have bought into his bullshit, haven't you?"

"All I know is he pays well."

"Yeah and look at how things have changed over the past year. Since he started using, we have come this close to being nabbed by the cops. I swear, I'm not doing time for that asshole. Good pay or not, there are others in Anchorage who run operations that are smart. This is reckless. You have to admit. No one in their right mind would take an entire building hostage."

"It's barely eighty people."

"Still. He's putting all of us at risk."

"And you're getting paid well."

The other guy continued grumbling as they searched. Alex looked at Kip who took out a piece of gum, peeled off the wrapping and stuck it in his mouth. He was as cool as a cucumber.

"There is nothing here, let's get the hell out," the white guy said.

"Not until we tear this place apart."

"Really?"

"You see, you don't get it, do you, Raymond? The sooner we get through all of this, the sooner we get the hell out of here. You don't want to be here. Well neither do I but he's not going to leave until we have searched this place from top to bottom."

They swung open the large cage door that was already unlocked and made their way in. The only things separating them from Alex and Kip were multiple heavy cupboards. They opened them and started tossing clothes and artwork out onto the ground, creating a huge messy pile.

"I didn't sign up for this shit."

"Stop bitching."

The black guy moved around to work on the next cupboard and Alex could tell they were close to being caught. All he had to do was look down through the crack between the two cupboards and he would see them. Kip knew this too as he glanced at Alex and muttered the words, "Move around."

Alex shifted and moved out of view. However, there wasn't enough room for both of them. He was about to tell Kip to take his place when…

"Hey!" the black guy shouted.

Now had he known what Kip was going to do next he would have stopped him, or at least come to his aid, but it all happened so quick. Kip stood up and put his hands in the air.

"Don't shoot. I'm unarmed."

"Get out here now."

They raised their guns at him and Alex could only watch in horror through a thin crack. He heard the sound of cupboards being shifted and then Kip being shoved up against a wall.

"Anyone else back there?"

"No, I'm alone," he replied.

Alex didn't dare breathe or peek out from his hiding spot. He contemplated opening fire for a split second and he might have done so if it wasn't for the thought of harm coming to Jess and Hayley from his actions. It wouldn't help if both of them were caught. All he could do was listen as they dragged Kip out of there, forcing him towards the exit. Alex moved out and caught Kip glance back for a second before he disappeared around the corner. He waited a few minutes longer before making his way out and exiting the storage locker. He crossed the room fast, keeping his gun raised in expectation of being spotted. He heard their voices growing distant as they made their way up to the first floor. When he was certain it was safe to move, Alex took off to see where they were taking him.

* * *

Kip pushed back against the men as they shoved him down the hallway, occasionally striking him in the back with the butt of their guns. "Keep moving, old man."

They took him to where his store was and shoved him into the room. Inside there was a tall, slender man with stubble and hair swept back sitting behind his table with his feet up. He was chewing on an apple.

Kip's legs buckled as he was forced to his knees.

"There's no need for that. Get him up," the stranger said.

Hauled to his feet, he groaned feeling a shot of pain go from his leg up his back. He wasn't young anymore. Years gone by, he would have lashed out and taken a beating if need be, but that was when he was cocky and thought he could tackle anything that came his way. It was the same cockiness that had driven him into the Marines. Back then it was all about serving his country and protecting those he loved but his views had changed now that he was older, now that he'd seen the way the government had abandoned their veterans. Sure they had Veterans Day to honor those who had served but how did that help him pay his bills? How did that help him deal with the trauma of what he'd seen overseas? It was a joke. He loved the brotherhood and camaraderie but that was it.

"What do we have here?" the man said tossing his apple into a trash can across the room and swinging his legs off the table.

"Found him in the basement hiding behind storage lockers."

"Huh. Anyone else?"

"Nope, just him."

"You sure?"

"Positive."

He eyed Kip. "And who might you be?"

"The guy who fucked your mother," Kip replied showing his disdain for him. He spat near the guy's feet. There were a few things he wouldn't put up with and answering to an asshole who killed innocents was one.

"Cute."

The guy glanced at his shoulder tattoo. "Well lookie

here, wc havc a Marine. A badass Marine." He got real close to Kip. "I bet you've seen a lot of things in your time, haven't you, old-timer?"

"If you mean assholes like you. Yeah."

The guy smirked and walked over to the table and picked up a photo of his daughter, one sent to him years after her mother prevented him from having contact. It had been the only one he'd received, and it wasn't her mother who sent it but his daughter. They'd planned to see one another in a few months for the first time. She'd written to him and they'd spoken once over the phone but that was it.

"Your daughter?" the man asked.

Kip said nothing. He walked over to the wall and glanced at a framed article that Doug had given to him on his sixtieth birthday as a way of thanking him for all his help. They'd had a local news crew come down and chat to him, take his photo, and featured it in the local paper. He'd relished that.

The man squinted at the photo. "Kip Brown. The

owner of the Kozy Korner who also assists with maintenance. Well looks like you are famous, Kip. It also looks like you know your way around this building." He glanced back and smiled. "I'll assume you're familiar with the residents. Yes?"

Kip said nothing.

The man walked back over to him. "Greg Mitchell. You know him?" he asked. He waited for a response. When he didn't get it, he continued. "I'll take that as a yes. Well, you see, Kip, Greg had something of mine and I went to a lot of trouble to get it here only to have it go missing."

"The drugs," Kip replied.

"Oh, so you do know about it?"

"Of course."

The man got this wide grin on his face as he got closer. "Where is it?"

"Somewhere you won't get your hands on it."

He scoffed. "Look, I admit what you did for our country was admirable but…"

Before he finished, he spun and threw a punch into Kip's stomach causing him to heave and curl over. Cayden patted him on the back. "Come on, old man. I thought you Marines were tougher than that."

"You sonofabitch!" Kip spat.

"I'll ask again. Where is my package?"

"In this building,"

"Where?"

"That's for me to know and you never to find out."

"Gotta love this guy." Cayden hit him again, this time knocking him out of the room into the hallway. Kip collapsed onto the ground and coughed hard. He struggled to get up, looking down the hallway to the stairwell. Beyond the crack of the door he saw Alex. Kip shook his head ever so slightly to indicate not to do anything.

Cayden stepped out into the hallway, as did three of his men, guns trained on him. He crouched down and grabbed a hold of him by the back of the neck and launched two more strikes at his face, each one more brutal than the last. Blood dripped out of Kip's mouth in large droplets, staining the floor below.

"Last chance, old man. Where is it?"

Kip could have told him or he could have lied but there was nothing that riled him more than a self-entitled prick who thought he could waltz into his home and kill people for no other reason than greed. He wasn't going to give him the satisfaction, and he sure as hell wasn't going to tell him.

He twisted over onto his back gasping. He motioned with his hand for Cayden to come close as he mumbled under his breath. As Cayden got close, he lashed out and caught him on the edge of his chin, knocking him back before starting to laugh. Cayden spat blood from his mouth and got up off the ground, he removed his handgun and then jammed the muzzle into Kip's mouth.

"Where is it?" His voice boomed loudly.

He pulled it out and Kip managed to muster the words, "Fuck you!"

The gun erupted, and a round tore through his skull.

Chapter 11

The lights in the public safety building came back on and Ed Solomon breathed a sigh of relief. Deke Lewis, their guy who fixed any problem they had with technology, stood back from the generator. He was a barrel-chested man, with a round face and a permanent red nose from drinking one too many whiskeys. "There we go. We are up and running again. Let's hope it holds."

"Good job."

They headed back up to the first floor and glanced out the window.

"Scott, any sign of Alex yet?"

"Not so far. However, we have a major problem."

"Oh no, what now?"

"You need to see this."

Scott led him up to the third floor where the city council chambers were. It was a large room with a slanted roof, and lots of windows. There was a semi-circle table that was used by the council when they voted on issues and heard complaints. Scott led him over to the window and pointed.

His eyed widened. The bay of Prince William Sound had risen over the banks and was starting to flood the harbor and town. In all his years, through all the storms they'd encountered, he'd never seen it breach the docks. Boats that were once in slips were now floating in the parking lot as a huge wave crashed and flooded the streets and all the seafood shacks and small buildings closed for the season. What was also surprising to see was large pieces of ice being pushed inland.

"Holy shit."

"What do we do?" Scott asked.

They'd never encountered a situation like this before. Sure, the weather had got bad and there were many weeks when folks didn't venture out for fear of getting lost in a blizzard and freezing to death, but this was on a whole new level. Heavy snow and eighty mile an hour winds was one thing, but throw water into the mix and whatever communication they had to the outside world via the landlines would be gone.

"We need to evacuate."

"But the tunnel is closed," Scott said.

Solomon nodded and hurried over to the closest landline phone, positioned on a desk across the room. He scooped it up. There was still a dial tone. *Thank God!* He dialed in the number for AKRR dispatch in Anchorage. Even though he could override the gates with a key, they usually opened the tunnel remotely. They'd had to do it numerous times when there was an emergency and someone needed to be rushed to the hospital.

Someone picked up on the other end and he breathed a sigh of relief.

"Thank God. This is Chief Solomon of the Whittier Police Department. I need—"

Click. The line went dead.

"Hello. Hello?" he yelled and tried again to phone but this time there was no dial tone. Absolutely nothing. "Shit!" He slammed the phone down hard. "The line is out."

Scott backed up to the window and glanced out. "What about the airport?"

He shook his head. "There're no planes."

"But I saw one there this morning."

"It's not in operation. It belongs to Bud Jenkins and that old coot wouldn't let us near that even if it did work."

There was a small landing strip that was used for private planes but in the winter they rarely saw it used, and it was close to the harbor on the east side, which meant it was probably underwater by now. There were only two options, and that was to leave by boat or to head to the highest ground, which was Begich Towers. From there they would have to hope that the water would recede or the cold weather froze it.

He tried one more time to get through to Anchorage but the line was dead.

Without saying another word he took off to alert everyone else. That day there had only been a skeleton crew functioning. Most of the Whittier Fire Department and EMTs were volunteers, and they commuted in. With the extreme weather many didn't make it and the few that had braved the Arctic conditions weren't meant to start their shift until eight and by that time the tunnel had been closed. Apart from three police officers, one dispatcher, and two city officials there were only two workers from the fire department, and one EMT on hand.

Within minutes water started splashing up against the front and rear doors seeping in and covering the floor in a thin layer of water.

"Where's Parker?" Solomon asked.

"Before the lines went dead, he went out to the apartments on Blackstone Road to assist someone who called in to say the power was out and they needed help to get their grandmother to safety," Debbie said as she went and put her coat on in preparation to leave. A tiny percentage of Whittier lived in what was known as Whittier Manor, it was a low-rise condo that overlooked the railyard. Somewhere between ten and twenty families lived there, mostly fishermen and those working in the canning plant.

"All right. Gather what you can. Marty, see if you can find some boots and grab up the rain jackets." Marty Rollins was chief of the fire service, a large guy in his early thirties, well-built and had been through more than one big event in the town. "Someone grab the radio equipment. Debbie, get your things and let's go."

As they hurried collecting what they needed and making sure that no one else was in the building, the water rose to almost knee-deep outside. It was coming in faster than expected, wave after wave pushing inland, soaking and filling every inch of the town.

"How did it rise so quickly?" Scott asked.

Debbie shrugged looking petrified. Outside, the early afternoon light had vanished, overtaken by brooding dark clouds and a heavy fog that hung low at street level. If that wasn't bad enough, the snow continued to fall reducing visibility.

Their group stood by the door and Solomon gripped the handle. "You ready?"

They could see the water pressed up against the door and knew it was going to flood in the second they opened it wide. He pulled back the door and had to cling to the handle to prevent himself from losing his footing. Frigid waters rushed in, lapping up against the walls and their legs. Everyone braced themselves then began to move forward out into the cold. Bitter strong winds bit at their skin, trying to topple them over as they waded through what was quickly becoming knee-high water.

On a good day the distance between the Public Safety Department and Begich Towers was no more than a six-minute walk but with the water making it virtually impossible to move fast and the numerous obstacles in their path, that time would double.

Their voices were almost lost in the gale.

"What about Lucas?" Scott yelled. "We can't leave him out there."

"Okay, listen up," Solomon said turning towards the

rest of them. "Make your way to the towers. Scott and I will go and get Lucas. Marty, you want to lead the way?"

He nodded and made his way to the front, leading the rest of the group through the harsh blizzard. It couldn't have got any worse. Rising water, whiteout conditions and winds that felt like they were high up on a mountain were causing all manner of destruction and danger.

* * *

Inside the towers, Alex was in shock. He couldn't believe what he'd just witnessed. He didn't expect him to pull the trigger. As he climbed the stairs to the next floor, his mind was in turmoil. If it wasn't for the atrocities he'd witnessed over in the Middle East, he might have been inclined to hand over the bag but he knew that wouldn't have changed matters. His thighs burned as he climbed the steps, making his way to a place of perceived safety. He had no idea what to do other than to find somewhere to hide; somewhere he could gather his thoughts. He stopped on each floor to see if anyone was there. He made it to the third when he noticed it was clear. He shot out and entered the first apartment to his right. He closed the door and locked it and headed over to the window, gripping his gun tightly. His heart was pounding and his thoughts running rampant. As he looked out the window his mouth widened. Water was everywhere. It was as if the entire town's streets had turned into rivers.

Alex dropped down, pressing his back against the wall and holding the gun close to his chest. He tapped it a few times against his head. "Think. Think!"

Overwhelmed and unsure of what to do, he slowed his breathing.

His mind flashed back to Fallujah and when the platoon he was patrolling with came under attack from two of the Afghans that were meant to be helping them. They called it a green-on-blue attack — something that was becoming all too familiar in the Middle East. It was strange what kinds of thoughts went through his mind when pushed into stressful situations. Fortunately he didn't suffer from PTSD but that didn't mean he wasn't affected by what he'd seen. It haunted every soldier.

Alex unzipped the bag and looked inside. It was hard to imagine that people could go to such lengths for drugs. He zipped it up and rose to his feet. This was a situation for SWAT. A Glock certainly wasn't going to cut it. They were packing serious heat. Alex looked out into the wall of white. He squinted at the sight of tiny figures in the distance. He couldn't tell if it was people or logs floating across the water. Snow blew around in the air making it hard to see. Slowly but surely he could tell that it was a group heading their way. Their heads were bowed, and they were clinging to each other like school kids in a line as they pushed against the gale force winds and waded through the ever-increasing water. At first he felt a smidgen of hope. It had to be Solomon. Then it dawned on him. If they entered the building, there was a good chance they wouldn't survive. He unlocked the window and tried to pull it back but it was frozen solid. "C'mon, you bastard!"

After witnessing what little impact a steel fire extinguisher did to the glass in the basement, he didn't even bother to try using a chair. All he could do was look on as they got closer. *Try the next apartment,* he thought.

He hurried out, pausing only to look both ways and listen for the men patrolling the hallways. Alex darted out and headed into the next apartment. Not wasting a second he tried again to open a window but it was frozen solid. The temperatures had dropped so dramatically overnight that it was pointless to keep trying.

He banged his fist against the window, despondent and overwhelmed.

All he could do was watch as the group got closer to the entrance.

They climbed the steps and began pounding on the doors.

Seconds turned into minutes and those closest to the entrance took a few steps back. Were they giving up? Had the men inside flashed their guns? It didn't matter because if they stayed out there any longer they were going to die. He watched as a hard wind blew into them forcing them up against the steel railing. In the distance,

Alex saw a huge surge of water push in from the bay, filling up the streets even faster and causing the water to rise higher.

It didn't take long to reach the Begich building. When it hit, the group braced themselves against the railing — a pointless endeavor. Within seconds two of them were washed away, carried off by the dark waters. One second they were above the surface and the next, gone. The remaining survivors could do nothing except cling to the railing for dear life. One of them pushed his way up and banged on the doors but they weren't answering. No one was getting in, and no one would get out.

Another sudden surge of water battered them and hands gave way, and the remaining group were forced off the steps and down into the streets, bobbing up and down until they could no longer tread water.

Alex watched the last one vanish and his heart sank.

He slowly banged on the glass, letting out his frustration.

What hope lay beyond the building was gone, at least

from what he could tell. He pushed away from the window, distraught and lost in the weight of the situation. Dealing with these assholes was hard enough with a team but without assistance what hope did they have? He considered for a moment handing over the bag and rolling the dice on what Kip had said. There was no telling if it would work or not but something told him not to. Call it a gut instinct gained from years of facing the enemy. He opted to hold on to the heroin in the hope of using it as a bargaining tool.

First things first, he would divide it up, so in the event he was caught he'd still have some leverage, as right now that was all he had going for him.

Chapter 12

Despite Whittier's many flaws, there was one upside to living in a harbor town — an abundance of vessels. The damn things were everywhere. Large yachts, modest fishing boats, through to kayaks. The ones that had been taken out of the water and placed on trailers were okay but smaller boats were floating in the streets. The cold water was now up to his waist and had made the lower half of his body numb. Shivering, they reached Prince William Sound Kayak Center which was surrounded by vessels. They cleared off heavy snow from the top of a boat cover, before peeling the cover back and entering the 12-foot aluminum boat. He got in first and extended a hand to Scott. Both of them were losing body heat fast and were liable to die if they didn't find somewhere warm. They'd underestimated the cold, the water level, and the weather that was getting worse.

Once Scott climbed in they lay back looking up at the

overcast sky, grateful for even the slightest bit of relief. Solomon's lips had turned a light shade of blue and his teeth were chattering. The snow continued to fall, thick and heavy with a fast westerly wind sweeping up icy needles in their faces. Solomon gasped and shivered again, he couldn't stop. The boat bobbed in the water and Solomon told Scott to put on one of the lifejackets in the front while he tried to get the motor running. His fingers were in so much pain from the cold he could barely clench a fist. He squeezed the ball on the fuel line to get some gas in the motor, then pulled the choke out, and made sure it was in neutral. He yanked on the cord to start the engine and it spluttered, he tried again and this time it started. Solomon let the engine warm up for a couple of minutes before he pushed the choke in. He pushed the lever to put it into reverse and backed it up before tearing away through the water heading for Whittier Manor.

The water churned up behind the boat leaving a wake that was white and frothy.

The boat powered down Eastern Avenue before they turned onto Depot Road with the plans of going around to Blackstone Road. They couldn't have gone past the Buckner building as it was up on a steep incline and the water hadn't yet risen that high so they headed on hoping to sweep around the far side.

Solomon gawked at how much of the town was now underwater. The railroad couldn't even be seen and there was no defining line between the bay and the town except for areas that were closer to the foot of the mountain. As they brought the boat around onto Blackstone, they heard Parker long before they saw him.

"Hey!" his voice bellowed. "Over here."

As they couldn't get close enough because the water still hadn't reached the apartment level they stopped and beckoned him to come down.

"No, we're good. Come on up."

"They want us to get back in the water? Are they mad?" Scott asked.

Solomon turned off the motor and rolled out into the

frigid waters. "Right now all I care about is getting warm."

"But they don't have any power."

"C'mon," Solomon said tugging a rope at the end of the boat and tying it off around a tree. Scott eased out of the boat and they waded through the water until they made it onto higher ground where it was dry. They were met at the entrance of the two-story green and cream apartments.

Parker brought out with him Ted Manning, a local fisherman and several thermal blankets. He and Ted covered them and ushered them into a house. While it wasn't warm it was dry and out of the howling winds. Ted struggled to shut his front door and had to press his body against it before he could lock it. Once inside Parker started yakking. Lucas Parker had been with the department for close to fifteen years. He was usually first on scene if there was an issue and extremely good at talking people down from a ledge. He'd originally been an EMT so his familiarity with troubling situations made him a perfect candidate for the police.

"Ted, grab some more blankets. You guys are going to need to get out of those clothes before you come down with pneumonia."

"You okay?" Solomon asked.

He chuckled. "You're asking me? I'm fine. At least I'm dry."

"I told you not to go out."

Lucas's brow pinched together. "And leave these people?"

"How many are still here?"

"Some of them left when they saw the water getting close. Did you see anyone out there?" Ted asked returning with more blankets.

Solomon shivered and shook his head. "Nope. The water is still rising. We won't be able to stay here much longer."

"It's going to take a while to get up to this level."

"You'd be surprised. It was ankle deep for about ten minutes, then a huge wave took it up to waist level," Scott said. Ted went across the room and pulled out a bottle of bourbon and poured two fingers into glasses before handing them over.

"Get that down you."

Solomon winced after knocking it back. "Oh that's good," he said.

"Another?" Ted asked.

Scott nodded. "So what do you know about this storm, Ted?"

"Why are you asking me?"

"You fish these waters. It's your job to know," Scott said.

While he poured out another he continued talking. "Look, the weather forecast for the week didn't look like anything out of the ordinary. This is as much a mystery to me as it is to you."

"I know someone who might know," Solomon said.

Lucas chimed in. "Don't say Kip. That guy has all manner of things rattling around in his brain."

"Actually I wasn't going to say that. I was referring to

Bud Jenkins."

"Yeah, right. He's probably washed away like the rest of those people out there."

"Not Bud," Solomon said. "If anyone could survive this it would be him."

"Oh because he's a prepper or because he's mentally unstable?" Ted laughed as he brought back their glasses. Solomon downed his. He was starting to feel better. The cold chilled him to the bone but being out of the wind was helping. He peeled out of his wet clothes and Ted took them to squeeze out the water.

"Not much point you doing that. We'll have to get back in the water if we want to help those over at the towers."

"Help them?" Ted asked standing at the foot of his stairs. "If these waters rise anymore we need to leave. There's no time to save people."

Solomon looked up at him. "There are young kids, seniors, and families in that building. Besides, I've got another officer out there. I'm not leaving him."

Ted scoffed. "Oh him. Yeah, heard about the new addition. I bet he wished he'd gone elsewhere now. Like they say…"

"Don't say it, Ted," Scott said.

"No place shittier than Whittier."

Scott groaned and pulled the blankets around him tighter.

"You two might want to cuddle each other," Ted said.

"What?" Scott shot back.

"To get your circulation moving. Go on, Lucas, get in there and give them a rubdown."

Lucas tossed him the bird and Ted laughed as he trudged up the stairs.

"Lucas, how many others are here?" Solomon asked.

"Like he said, they're gone. The old lady who I originally came for died. By the time I got here she was already out cold."

"Seniors will be the first to go," Scott said. "We're going to see more of that by the end of the night."

"I hope not," Lucas said. "I had to pull Jamie away

from his grandmother. I tried to console the guy but he took off. Haven't seen him since." He pulled out a packet of cigarettes and banged one out.

"I thought you'd given that up," Solomon said.

"That vape shit you recommended was terrible," Lucas replied, puffing away.

They sat there in the silence warming up for close to twenty minutes.

"Wasn't there a generator in this place?" Scott asked.

"Should have been," Lucas said. "But there wasn't. Seems the owner thought it was an unnecessary cost."

"For Whittier?" Scott asked. "Crazy."

"By the way where are the others?" Lucas asked

"They headed over to Begich Towers."

Lucas nodded and leaned back in a recliner chair. "Probably the best place to be right now. Highest place in Whittier besides the mountain."

"Well that's the thing, I was going to manually open the four gates in the tunnel but with all this water, there's no point. Our best bet is to head over there, reassure the families and hunker down until this storm passes."

* * *

Knowing they had already searched through the lower rooms, Alex rooted around in the apartment for a bag, any bag he could use to divide up the drugs. He found a grocery bag and threw four bricks into it, then looked around for a place to stash it. It was going in the ceiling but he wanted it in an area where it wouldn't be easily found. Entering the bedroom he walked over to the closet and looked inside. He pulled over a chair and hopped up onto it and pushed up a tile and squeezed the bag into place, then closed it and stepped back to make sure nothing looked out of place.

Satisfied he backed out of the room. As he did he stepped on a mirror that had been overturned and it shattered below his boots. In the seconds after, he heard a voice, then boots running down the hallway. Alex's nostrils flared as he hurried to find a place to hide. He ducked down behind an overturned sofa and lay quietly as the person entered the apartment. Right then he noticed he didn't have the duffel bag over his shoulder. It was at the far end of the sofa, with the zipper undone.

"You might as well come out," a gruff voice said.

Twisting ever so slightly so he could see the bag, he tried to move towards it to pull it out of the way. His breathing became rapid, and he knew this guy wasn't walking out of here until he'd performed his search. Using a piece of broken mirror, Alex lifted it to try and get a bead on the guy. He couldn't see anything. He could hear him and roughly judge where he was but each time he tried there was no one there.

A door was kicked and in the seconds after, Alex stuck up the piece of mirror above the sofa and then brought it back down. Sure enough he was on the far side of the room about to enter the bathroom. Alex shuffled along behind the sofa and waited until he entered the bathroom to toss the bag across the room. It hit the ground landing somewhere in the middle of the room, zipper open, drugs exposed. Still using the shard of mirror he watched as the man darted out expecting to find someone only to glance down and see the bag. His eyes widened and a smile came across his face. That momentary distraction was all Alex needed. He wheeled around the sofa and fired two rounds; one struck him spinning him to the ground. Alex darted up and was heading for him when he unleashed a flurry of rounds back that peppered the wall behind him. Hitting the tiled floor on his knees, he fired three more rounds, each one hitting its mark, ending his pitiful life.

Without a second to lose, he scooped up the guy's gun, any ammo he had on him, his radio and the duffel bag and darted out of there heading for the stairwell.

The gunfire would have easily been heard.

Sure enough, the very moment he entered the stairwell he heard the door open on the level below. Alex ascended the steps keeping his back against the wall.

Chapter 13

In an empty apartment on the fifteenth floor, Cayden unleashed his fury. He upended a table, rammed a lampstand into a cupboard, and smashed a chair against the wall. Leon looked on thinking it was hilarious. The guy was coming apart at the seams and yet he refused to listen to anyone. Cayden stopped destroying furniture and pulled out a small baggie of coke and created a line on the table. He rolled a hundred-dollar bill and snorted it up.

"Are you done?" Leon asked.

Cayden scowled at him as he wiped the white powder from below his nose and looked out the window. He banged his fist slowly against the window. It was just the two of them in the apartment.

"It's in here. I know it is."

"What the hell has happened to you, man?" Leon asked.

"Nothing."

"Bullshit. You never used to be this way. It's like you're driven by some kind of demon."

Cayden snorted.

"I'm serious. It's not like you're hurting for money. You could walk away from all of this and never have to work again in your life."

"Are we back to that again, Leon?"

"Yeah, we fucking are! How about for once you stop pushing the topic to one side and actually address it? You remember when we were kids?"

"Of course I do."

"Do you remember us saying if we ever made a million we would stop working and go enjoy life?"

He groaned. "We were too young, Leon. We had no concept of money. A million dollars doesn't get you anywhere in this world."

"Well how much does? Five, ten, a hundred? At what point do you think it's okay to slow down and stop chasing the money? Can't you see what it's doing to you?"

"What's it doing to me, Leon, huh?" Cayden asked walking over to the sofa, slumping down and pulling out a metal canister. He screwed off the top and took a swig before offering Leon some. It was his own personal flask of bourbon that he was in the habit of carrying around.

"It's destroying you. You've lost your marriage and your kid."

"She was cheating on me," Cayden said.

"I wonder why? Huh? You ever thought of that? You spend all your time chasing the next big deal and acting as though if you don't get to the next one the world is going to cave in on you, but you don't realize it already has. We never signed up for this. We said we would get in, make our money and get out. That was always the agreement."

"Agreement? Shit, Leon, we were just kids. We had no idea of the responsibilities."

"Fuck the responsibilities. You have paid your dues, you've done your time. We aren't getting any younger, Cayden, and I certainly don't want to end up spending the rest of my days behind bars."

"It won't happen."

"Like you didn't expect this to happen?"

"That's different, Greg was an asshole I shouldn't have trusted him," he said pulling a pack of Marlboro Lights from his pocket and tapping one out.

"And what about all the others you're trusting? Who's to say they won't turn on you?" Leon asked.

Cayden smiled. "They wouldn't dare."

Leon stared back and shook his head. "You've bought into your own hype. I don't even recognize you anymore."

"Oh shut the fuck up, Leon."

Leon walked over to the window and pressed his head against it looking down at the rising waters. "Have you seen it out there?" He sighed. "It's getting worse. We need to leave."

"No one is fucking leaving this place until I have my package."

"Shit, Cayden. That guy was probably messing with you. Do you really think it's in this building?"

Cayden turned in his seat and had a dead serious expression across his face.

"You didn't look in that guy's eyes before pulling the trigger. He was willing to die to keep that information from me. Now I gotta ask myself why would someone do that? Why wouldn't they just tell me?"

"Maybe because you sucker punched him in the gut, stuck a gun in his face?"

"Leon, you are starting to worry me. Next thing you'll be telling me is you've found God. Well? Have you? As you sure seem to talk a lot about how you don't recognize me but you're acting all out of sorts. It's beginning to disturb me."

Leon shook his head. "There's no point talking to you. You'll keep going until you land flat on your face."

Cayden studied him and for a second Leon thought he was about to explode but instead he said, "Okay. You tell me then what you expect me to do?"

That caught Leon off guard. He hadn't got a response out of Cayden like that since they were in their late teens.

Back then he always bounced ideas off him and sought his advice over difficult situations. "I don't expect you to do anything. I just don't want to see you go over the edge and right now you are teetering on it. The drug use. The alcohol. All these snap decisions. The kinds of deals you are setting up. The lack of slowing down. You are on a collision course with death, and as your friend, I'm asking you to stop and think. Is it all worth it?"

"It's sixty million dollars, Leon."

"And?"

"And I have deals that are already set up. Clients who were waiting. What do I tell them?"

"You don't tell them anything. You hand them back their money and walk away."

He scoffed. "Walk away. You make it sound so easy but you know as well as I do, you don't walk away from this."

There was a long pause then Leon replied, "You might not have any choice. Even if you find this package, do you think we are getting out of here? Have you seen it out there?" He pointed to the window and walked back. "You saw what happened to those people."

"So we wait for the water to recede."

"And if it doesn't?"

Cayden began looking flustered. The coke was kicking in and overtaking his common sense. It was always the same. One minute he was level-headed and open to talk and the next flying off the handle and looking antsy.

"It will. It's a bad storm. That's all. We've had them before."

"Not like this we haven't."

Cayden walked over and looked out. "There are boats in this town. Once we have that package, we sail out of here and head back to Anchorage."

Leon laughed. "Okay, Cayden. Okay. Let's do it your way. It's not like you listen to me."

Cayden grabbed a hold of him and pushed him up against the window. "I'm at the helm of his ship. Don't treat me like an idiot."

"Get off me," Leon said in a calm voice. "You might

throw your weight around with others but it doesn't work on me. I see through that crap." Leon pushed him and began to walk towards the door. That's when he heard the sound of a gun cocking. He froze and turned ever so slightly. Cayden was standing with a Beretta aimed at him.

Leon scoffed. "Huh. You going to shoot me?"

"I haven't decided."

He walked back to him and stood right across from the barrel and then grabbed it and placed it against his forehead. "I've known you since you were a kid. You want to shoot. Go ahead. Get rid of the final piece of your pitiful fucking life. Cause you've already done a great job with the little you had."

"Don't push me, Leon."

"Go on! Squeeze the fucking trigger, Cayden, or get this thing out of my face."

There was a tense few seconds as they stared at each other. Before a decision was made, there was a knock at the door and Vic entered. His eyes bounced between them.

“Uh, I’ll come back.”

“Stay where you are,” Cayden said pulling the gun away. It left a mark on Leon’s forehead. He slipped the gun back into the small of his back and looked away from Leon. “What is it?”

“We’ve got a problem. Chris is dead.”

“What?” Cayden stammered.

“Found his body on the third floor. He wasn’t responding over the radio. Someone shot him.”

Cayden glanced at Leon and both of them stormed out of the room heading for the elevator. As the elevator descended he continued to pepper Vic with questions. “Was there anyone with that old guy when you found him? Have you checked all the rooms? How did you overlook this?”

Cayden preferred to blame others than take responsibility.

The fact was they were in this mess because of him, because of greed, and because of his inability to think clearly. The drugs had clouded his judgment and made him rash in his decisions. When the elevator opened on the third floor they hurried down to the room where several of the other guys were waiting. Cayden brushed past them and glanced at Chris's body. Chris had been a good friend of Cayden's. He was the youngest in their crew and Cayden had taken him under his wing and treated him like he was his brother. At one time Leon had asked him why he spent so much time with Chris and his reply was simple… "because he reminds me of myself at that age."

Cayden dropped to a knee and placed a hand on Chris's chest.

"I'm going to speak with the rest of the group. Someone must know who did this. I want a list of names of the residents in this building. I want whoever did this found."

He ran his hand over Chris's face and closed his eyelids. Leon saw the muscles in Cayden's jaw clench, and one of his hands ball. He got up and looked around.

"That's not all, boss," Vic said turning to Jerome who handed him a brick of heroin. "We found this in one of the apartments under one of the tables."

Cayden stared at it, a look of glee in his eye. He turned to Leon and shook it in his face. "I told you. I told you it was here. Whoever did this must have the rest. I want this person found and now!"

He stormed out of the room and headed up to begin collecting names.

* * *

Alex kept only one brick of heroin on him for proof, the rest he stashed away in various apartments on the seventh, eighth and tenth floor. If he was caught, he would have a solid reason for them not to kill him. He was planning on using it as a negotiating tool. He'd want them to release some residents in exchange for the location of the drugs. He would repeat this process until everyone was out. Of course until then he would kill as many of them as he could to dwindle down their crew. Right now he didn't know how many there were, but at least he had a radio and could listen in on their conversations. He hurried out of the last apartment on the tenth floor for the stairwell, checking both ways before entering. His thoughts were all over the place as he tried to figure out where to go before starting the negotiation process. It had to be somewhere they were less likely to search. Somewhere that put their lives at risk. He glanced up the stairwell and listened to see if anyone was coming as he was sure he heard the sound of boots. It wasn't coming from above but below. Not wasting any time he ascended until he made it to the fifteenth floor. He peeked out the door and saw several armed men standing near the homeowners lounge. The stairwell went up one more flight to the roof. He had no other choice than to head onto the roof.

Alex struggled to push the roof door open due to the heavy winds. He slipped out and hung on for dear life as Mother Nature tried to force him off. These were no ordinary winds. These had to be reaching speeds of more than 80 mph. He couldn't just make a run to one of the many steel air vents that stuck up out of the roof. The wind was too strong. Then again he couldn't stand in the doorway. He could hear the men climbing the stairs. Seconds. That's all he had. Pushed into a corner, he felt his heart race. What to do? The heavy sound of boots getting closer, and clear conversation made the decision for him. He took a deep breath and released his grip on the roof's door and lunged forward racing for an air vent. It was like running on an ice rink. Heavy snow had fallen covering the roof, freezing cold temperatures had turned the snow into something as slick as black ice. His feet gave out from underneath him as the wind veered him off course away from the vent and towards the edge of the building. He gasped, realizing that he was seconds away from being blown off the high-rise.

As he tried to brace himself that only made it worse.

Alex toppled, spinning and turning over until he hit the lip of the building. He clasped hold of the steel just as the wind pushed him over the edge. His stomach dropped at the sight of the ground far below. His fingers clung to the steel lip for dear life. He used every ounce of strength he had to hold on as the wind batted him like a rag doll. It didn't help that ice had formed on the metal making it even more slippery. He knew he couldn't hold himself up for much longer and if he didn't get up now, he'd drop.

Like performing a chin-up he hauled his body into the onslaught of the merciless wind. He clambered over staying as low as he could and digging his nails into the shingles. Like a spider clinging on for dear life, he crawled and inched his way forward towards the closest air vent.

It didn't help that every second he was out there his body was losing heat. Shivering and in pain from the cold he worked his way over to one of the air vents and got behind it. Alex remained there for a few minutes to catch his breath as the wind sliced around him as a constant reminder that if he stepped out he might die. The reality was if he didn't get off that roof, he would die.

Chilled to the bone and exhausted he knew returning to the stairwell was his only means of survival. Fear gripped him at the thought of falling to his death. The wind didn't seem to let up. He couldn't wait any longer. It was now or he'd freeze to death. Alex took a few deep breaths willing his mind to relax. His heart was pounding in his chest as he glanced around the steel vent. There was no way in hell he was going to be able to claw his way across the roof, it was too far away, and he couldn't make a straight run for it as the wind would push him off course. He took into account the force of the wind and decided to use it to his advantage. Instead of running towards the door he would head about ten feet to the left of it knowing that the wind would knock him towards the door.

Get a grip. You can do this! Alex launched himself away from the vent into the blizzard conditions and pounded the roof. His legs hammered like pistons. Sure enough the wind pushed him off course causing him to run straight into the doorway. He clasped hold; the blast almost lifted his feet off the ground. Twisting and pulling the knob he barely made it inside before the door slammed closed.

Alex fell to his knees, out of breath, frozen but alive.

Chapter 14

Solomon slipped into some dry clothes taken from one of the abandoned condo apartments. It felt good to feel warm. Ted had attempted to dry out his uniform but it was soaked. Beyond the pane of glass the wind howled as he pulled on a thick top. Outside water continued to rise and the urgency to leave increased. Scott entered the room. "You ready to go?"

"Not really but we have little choice."

Scott leaned against the wall; color had flooded his cheeks once again.

"Let's say everything goes well and we manage to extract everyone from the towers. Where next?"

"Depends on the waters. Depends on the extent of the situation. I say we head to Girdwood. It's the closest and hopefully with them being so far inland, maybe it'll be dry. If not there, Anchorage."

Scott pushed away from the wall and looked down at

his outfit. He had a smile on his face. "The duty belts look a little odd with those civilian clothes, don't you think?"

He nodded but his mind was too preoccupied. Solomon walked out and headed downstairs. Water had seeped in under the door and was about five inches deep. "Ted, did you get those flares of yours?"

He held up a bag.

Solomon was about to question him regarding his boat when there was a hard thump outside. All of them looked towards the door. There was another, it sounded like someone was knocking on doors farther down. Lucas trudged over in knee-high boots and looked out. "I don't see anyone."

Boom. Another thud, this time against their door. Lucas pulled it open and peered out only to have a man's limp body slump in front of him.

"Marty?" Solomon said hurrying over. "Give me a hand, Lucas." They scooped him up and dragged him in. He was out of breath and shivering like mad. They carried him upstairs and began stripping off his soaking wet clothes. Ted grabbed the insulated blankets and they wrapped every inch of his body. Marty's face was almost blue, his lips twitched and his eyes rolled back in his head as Solomon and Lucas tried to warm him up. Scott began rubbing his legs, while they worked the arms. Ted got behind him in a seated position so his body would be pressed up against his own, he rubbed furiously up and down his chest and belly. Marty tried to say something but it came out as a stutter because of the cold. They continued to work on him in silence for what felt like half an hour before he was able to speak. His teeth continued to chatter.

"What happened, Marty?"

"At the towers… mmmen."

Solomon's brow pinched and he looked at the others wondering if they understood what he said. "What?"

"I think he said men," Ted said.

"I know that, what did he mean?"

"Gggg… guns," Marty said. He shivered hard and his

eyes kept closing.

"Lucas, go grab some more blankets."

"There aren't any more insulated ones."

"It doesn't matter. Get anything."

Lucas disappeared out of the room and they heard him slam the door. The sound of water lapping up against the walls downstairs could be heard.

"Chief, we can't stay here," Scott said.

"I'm not letting him die."

Lucas returned a few minutes later, out of breath but with an armful of blankets. He dumped them down and they took off the wet ones they had and replaced them and continued to fold more over him. Unlike themselves, who had only experienced water up to their waists, Marty had been submerged. His hair had hardened and was covered in icicles, as were his eyebrows. Solomon told him not to talk but just to rest. He didn't want to put any more strain on his body than was essential. Right now he was in a fight for his life. Tired from rubbing his limbs but pleased to see some color come back into his face, they left him with Ted and ventured out into the hallway. Lucas leaned back against the wall, Scott hopped up onto the banister and Solomon paced — it kept the blood moving.

"What do you think he meant?" Scott asked.

"Men. Guns. Seems pretty straightforward," Lucas replied.

Solomon walked to the end of the hallway and looked out at the water sloshing around the evergreen trees that were weighed down by a thick layer of snow. Ice formed in areas where the water wasn't flowing and vehicles were nearly submerged with just the roofs appearing above the water. The condominium itself was up on a rise from Blackstone, but had it been on the same level as the road, the first floor would have been filled with water. Right now it was only ankle-deep on the ground floor. He glanced at the boat they arrived in still tied to the tree. It moved with the flow of the water. He thought back to his conversation with Danny on the day he took his life. He remembered Danny telling him about heroin and promising to take him to where it was. Had men shown up to find it? That was the only logical explanation. Sure, fishermen owned rifles but what reason would they have to be flashing them around?

"Chief?" Lucas asked.

Still lost in thought, he didn't hear him.

"Chief?" Lucas said again. This time he turned.

"What?"

"We need to head out."

"I know." He headed back into where Marty was and sat down beside him. His eyes were closed and his breathing was shallow but he had finally found his voice.

"Marty."

His eyes opened. "Hey, chief."

"What happened to the others?"

"Swept away. I tried to help but I couldn't hold on."

He squeezed his hand reassuringly. "And the towers?"

"There are armed men inside. They refused to open."

"Who are they?"

"I don't know. Haven't seen them around these parts."

His brow furrowed. “Anyone alive?”

“I think I saw someone dead on the ground.”

Solomon stared back blankly. He hadn’t told anyone in the department about his conversation with Danny out of respect to his father and the reputation of the department. The media would have eaten it up and as it stood Danny was being hailed as a hero for preventing Greg from opening fire on residents. The town treated the situation very black and white and he intended to keep it that way. Besides, there was the fact that he wasn’t sure if there was any truth to the existence of heroin. He could have taken sniffer dogs through the apartments but that would have only caused more questions and an internal investigation and he’d seen how those went. No, he kept his cards close to his chest and hoped it would all be swept under the rug and forgotten within a matter of weeks. He hadn’t thought of the complications that could arise from drugs not having been delivered. Were these the same men that Danny had been speaking to on the phone? He recalled him promising to deliver a package.

Was that it? And if so, had they shown up to collect? He reached up and squeezed the bridge of his brow feeling a headache coming on. "How many men were there?" he asked.

"I only saw three but there could have been more."

"And the doors?"

"Locked."

Without knowing the situation and how many they were up against, it would have been insane to go in. And how would they get in if the doors were locked? Behind him he heard a shuffle and turned to see Scott and Lucas in the doorway.

"Armed men?" Lucas asked.

"We're not going there, are we, chief?" Scott asked.

"We um..."

Lucas stepped forward. "We can't control the situation. If there were more of us maybe but under these conditions... We need to leave. Hopefully tomorrow the water will have receded and we can bring SWAT in from Anchorage."

"And what if the water doesn't recede, huh?" Solomon asked.

Lucas shrugged. "Not everyone is saved in a disaster."

Solomon narrowed his eyes. "Are you kidding me? These are friends, neighbors, good folk we live alongside. I'm not leaving them in that situation," Solomon replied.

"You heard him, the place is locked down. Even if we could get in, there are only five of us and three that are trained for these kinds of situations."

"I can shoot a gun," Ted said.

"And I can cook but that doesn't mean I'm good at it," Lucas replied.

"No one is getting left behind," Solomon said rising to his feet. "Now there is another way in but chances are it's submerged below water."

Lucas shook his head and walked out of the room. "We are not entering the towers through the school. That underground passage has to be filled by now. Besides it's close to sixty yards long."

"The building is far back and on a rise, there is a

chance the water hasn't filled it yet."

"Okay and what if we manage to get in? What's your big plan then? From what I know all we have is a few Glock 22's and a couple of shotguns in our vehicles, which I might add are now submerged."

"There are more shotguns back at the department, and diving gear."

"Oh my God. Chief, c'mon, there are times when going beyond duty is required, this is not one of them. We are talking about our lives here."

"Lucas, do you recall what your instructors told you when you were at the academy? Do you remember what you signed up for?"

"Yes. And I also remember them telling us that our safety was important as well."

There was a long pause as they looked at each other.

"Lucas. I don't have the time or the energy to sit here and argue with you. There is a job that needs to be done. People need helping. Now if you want to find a boat and get the hell out of here, then by all means, I won't hold it against you but I'm going in with or without you."

Solomon rose and scooped up his duty belt and wrapped it around his waist and secured it in place.

"And Marty?" Scott asked.

"Ted, you think you can look after him?"

"Here?"

"No, we'll get you to your boat and then just wait for us."

"And what if you don't return?"

"If we're not back by tomorrow morning or the weather gets worse, I expect you to leave, we'll find our own way out."

He nodded and Solomon brushed past Lucas as he exited. Scott and Ted helped Marty down the stairs and carried him above the small amount of water that had managed to make its way now into the first floor of the apartments. Outside, they forged their way through the brutal blizzard and down a steep incline back into the water and over to the tied-up boat. Solomon rolled into the boat and the others kept Marty out of the water, holding him up above their heads until they got him inside the boat. One by one they got in and then Solomon cranked the engine to life and it spluttered out of there. All of them kept their heads low as the wind tried to steer them out across the bay. Solomon gave the throttle a hard twist and the engine's propeller cut through the water leading them towards a graveyard of boats. They slalomed around many that had sunk, and many that were unmanned until they located Ted's.

Many bodies were floating on top of the water. He recognized the faces of the staff of the local donut depot. His stomach sank. On the way across town he thought about what Lucas had said and going beyond the call of duty. Sure, they didn't owe anyone in this town anything and people would understand if they took off but in some small way Solomon felt responsible — not for the storm but for the armed men.

His ex-wife, Natalie, had always told him that he put his job before anything else. It was the reason why she walked away, that and the fact that she couldn't stand to live in a town that was so isolated. She'd grown up in the big city and had always envisioned a life close to her family where she could depend on her mother and father for help, while Solomon had a different upbringing — one in which he was taught to stand on his own two feet and not depend on anyone. Perhaps that's why he'd excelled in his law enforcement career. Sure, he depended on fellow officers but that was different. Once his shift was over he didn't have any of them telling him how to live his life.

He glanced towards Begich Towers that loomed like a beast out of the snowy fog. He couldn't let those people down. He had enough on his conscience.

"There it is," he said pointing through the loose snow that was lifted and blown by the wind. In the distance was a thirty-foot white charter boat with a blue stripe down the side. It had the word Beth on the back, the name of Ted's late wife. When he wasn't fishing he was taking tourists around the bay. It was very profitable in the summer. Ted didn't have to worry about family as his wife had passed away ten years earlier from breast cancer and they'd never had kids. For someone that had experienced loss he never acted like a victim. He was one of the most cheerful guys Solomon knew. Always had a kind word. Always respected the police and efforts made by those in the town.

Solomon pulled up alongside the boat and killed the engine. Scott gripped the rope hanging to the side of Ted's boat and Lucas and Ted raised Marty up and onto his boat. Within a matter of minutes both of them were safely onboard.

"Remember," Solomon said. "If we are not back by the morning. If the waters keep rising. You get the hell out, okay?

He nodded. "Chief. Be careful out there," Ted said.

Solomon raised a thumb and fired up the engine. They took off heading for the police department to collect more firepower and ammo.

Chapter 15

Residents were allowed to go to the bathroom one at a time, anyone who wished to go while someone was using the single toilet had to wait, no exceptions. Jess knew if they stayed in that room they had no chance of surviving. Two of the four armed men watching over the group in the homeowners lounge had been gone for over ten minutes. Something was happening because she'd heard the guy they referred to as Cayden give them strict orders not to leave the room. The other two had closed the door and were out in the hallway. Every few minutes they would open the door and make sure everyone was still sitting on the floor.

As soon as the door was closed some of them would stand and look out the window and had already begun to discuss working together to overwhelm the two outside.

"I'm telling you it's possible," Ken Rogers said.

"And so is getting killed," an elderly woman shot back.

"You're not jeopardizing my life. If we stay here and do as they say, we have a good chance of surviving."

"Surviving? We've seen their faces," Ken replied.

"So what do you expect us to do? We are unarmed," someone else said.

"The passengers of Flight 93 were unarmed when they charged the cockpit," Ken continued.

"Yeah and I don't have to remind you how that turned out."

"The plane was out of control," Ken said.

"This is out of control," another person added.

"I'm with you," Jess said. Ken turned, a look of surprise on his face.

"Really?"

"Yeah, I mean what are the odds they are going to let us live?"

He stabbed the air and turned up his nose at the rest of them. "Exactly!" After, he looked back at her. "Sorry, I didn't catch your name?"

"Jess Riley," she turned, "and this is my daughter

Hayley."

"Jess. Hayley. I'm Ken. Pleased to make your acquaintance. I run the post office on the first floor."

She nodded. "So what did you have in mind?"

"There's two of them. If we can just get one of their weapons, we stand a chance. If we can overwhelm both maybe we can fight back."

"Fight back?" The elderly woman laughed. "Ken, you are fifty years old."

"I was in the Navy."

"Yeah, scrubbing decks and singing karaoke in gay bars," she scoffed. "I've seen more fight in a Catholic priest."

"Ah put a sock in it, Agnes." Ken pointed to her. "Agnes here is in charge of the local gossip. Ain't that right, Agnes?"

She flipped him the bird. For someone who looked over seventy she sure was full of piss and vinegar. Agnes turned her back on him and leaned into a man who was obviously her husband. He had a hearing aid on and seemed oblivious to the dispute.

"I'm with you," another woman said from behind Ken.

He turned and smiled and reached for her hand. "Clara. Thank you."

That appeared to be enough to rally a few more in the room to help.

Clara looked at Jess then back at the door. "So how do you want to do this?" Clara asked.

"Um," Ken said rolling his bottom lip under his teeth. He looked eager but confused.

"He hasn't a clue," Agnes said. "You'll get us all killed. Stupid man."

"Don't listen to her," Ken said before the room went quiet.

A few minutes passed.

"I have an idea," Jess said.

They huddled around and she explained what she had in mind. There was no guarantee it was going to work and there was a potential it could backfire and they could get shot, but being as the outcome of their situation didn't look any better they opted to give it a try. At first there was some disagreement but eventually they followed Jess's lead. A member of the group went to the washroom. Jess approached the door and knocked on it. One of the armed men with a bald head responded.

"What do you want?"

"Bathroom is in use. My daughter needs to go."

He cast a glance at Hayley who was crossing her legs.

"She'll have to wait her turn."

"She's been waiting her turn for the last ten minutes."

The guy stuck his head around the corner and then told his buddy to keep an eye on her. Baldy walked over to the bathroom and banged on the door. "Hurry up in there."

"Sorry, I have IBS," came the reply.

He scowled and walked back. "You'll just have to wait."

"We already have, now unless you want piss all over the floor, just take us to the next apartment. I'm just a woman, it's not like I'm going to be a problem, am I?" She appealed to his ego. His eyes scanned her as if sizing her up.

He turned to his buddy, and he shook his head. "You heard what Cayden said."

"Mister, I really need to go," Hayley said, adding fuel to the flames.

He sneered and jerked his rifle towards the door. "Let's go."

Hayley slipped by him and Jess went to follow and he stopped her. "Not you. Just her."

"I'm her mother. I'm not letting her go alone."

"She'll be fine."

Jess looked at Hayley. This wasn't what she banked on. Hayley gave her a reassuring smile and headed down the hall towards the next apartment. The door was closed and from behind her she heard Agnes chuckle. "I told you it wasn't going to work."

* * *

The bald guy shoved Hayley forward into the

apartment and followed her in, closing the door behind him. She went into the washroom and closed the door, locking it. She pressed against the door for a second and could hear the man light a cigarette. Hayley went over to the toilet and made some noise to make it sound like she was going. She dropped the toilet seat and turned on the tap ever so slightly and then looked around the bathroom for anything she could use against him. Her father had never taught her how to use a weapon, neither had he shown her any form of self-defense. The odds were stacked against her but the one thing she had working for her was the element of surprise. He wouldn't expect a sixteen-year-old to attack. If she could catch him off guard, maybe just maybe she could get the gun away from him. Hayley sat on the toilet seat and noticed the shower curtain rod. She got up and touched it. It was made of metal and had two rubber ends. Quietly she pulled it down and removed the curtain, then took off one of the rubber ends to expose a flat but sharp end. The rod was around six feet in length.

She moved it around but then decided to put it back. What was she thinking? He would slap it out of her hand and then beat her to death.

There was a bang on the door.

"Hey, speed it up."

"Yeah, nearly done," she replied.

Her eyes darted around the room. There was a bottle of bleach on the floor. She considered the various ways it could be used to blind him. Spray it in his eyes and… she shook her head. No. It wouldn't work. She was beginning to talk herself out of it.

That's when she looked at the mirror, and an idea came to her. She removed her jacket and placed it against the mirror to deaden the sound and catch pieces. Then using her foot she tapped the flusher on the toilet. It gurgled and made strange noises, and at that exact moment she used her elbow to crack the mirror. She heard a crunch and then felt the mirror give way behind her jacket. Slowly she pulled away, catching a few shards. She didn't intend to use it herself. But if she gave it to her mother or one of the guys in the room, maybe they could make use of it. Acting quickly she used a piece to cut away some of the thick plastic shower curtain and then tied it around one end of the mirror. Once done she put her jacket on, stuck the shard into the back of her jeans making sure not to cut herself and then unlocked the door.

"I'm done."

His lip curled as he blew out smoke from the corner of his mouth. As she went to move by him he put his arm across blocking her path. "You're a good-looking girl."

She swallowed hard but didn't look at him. "Thank you."

Hayley ducked under his arm and he stuck his leg out. "Hold on. Hold on. Not so fast. What's the rush? It's not like there is anything to go back to, is there?"

She balled a fist. The guy was huge, towering over her.

"Go take a seat on the bed over there."

"I really should get back to my mother," she said trying to scoot by him.

The bald guy pressed his hand against her chest forcing her back against the wall. "But I was just about to have some fun."

"Please, mister, I'm just sixteen."

"In some countries that's the legal age of consent."

"Well I don't consent."

"Oh don't be like that."

He shoved her hard, and she tumbled over onto the floor. The guy removed the rifle around his chest and laid it against the wall and approached her. Hayley started backing up scrambling away, but he caught up with her and grabbed her ankle. "Stop squirming and come here."

She cried out as he yanked her leg and pulled her towards him and tried to unbutton her jeans but she fought back. She tugged at them trying to stop him but he slapped her with the back of his hand. He then started undoing his belt. He reached forward and pulled her towards him by her hair and was in the middle of telling her what he was going to do when Hayley reached around for the shard of mirror. Her fingers raked the floor, searching for it. It had fallen out when he'd yanked down her jeans ever so slightly. The guy continued undoing his pants and was leaning over to get near her when she latched on to the mirror and in one smooth motion wheeled around and stuck it in his neck. Blood sprayed against the wall, a fine mist which thickened as he let out a cry and yanked it out. Hayley scrambled out from underneath him and stood there horrified as the man struggled to get to his feet. He staggered and collapsed on the bed, gasping in the grip of fear. He tried to go for his rifle and she raced around him and scooped it up aiming at him. She had no idea how to use it other than to pull the trigger.

But thankfully she didn't need to do that.

Blood gushed out his neck and then he collapsed.

It happened so fast. One moment he was upright, his hand clasped over his neck, his finger gloved in blood, and the next lying on the ground bleeding out.

Hayley stood there for a second or two frozen by fear. She clutched the rifle in her hand looking down at it like some alien object. It felt heavy in her grasp as she backed up to the door keeping her eyes on the man as if he was going to come alive and attack her. Convinced he was dead, and with her hands shaking from adrenaline pumping through her, she stepped out into the corridor, holding the rifle in the direction of the Homeowners lounge.

The other guy wasn't there. He was gone.

In all the commotion she hadn't heard what had taken place.

Until she opened the door into the homeowners lounge, she assumed he was inside, alive. He was there lying on the ground in a pool of blood with several others hunched over him. Her mother turned and saw Hayley covered in blood and gripping the rifle.

* * *

"Hayley!" Jess hurried over and took the gun from her daughter's hand and laid it on the floor so she could check her. She ran her hands over her arms and body expecting to find a knife or gunshot wound but found nothing.

Hayley raised her hands. “I’m okay, Mom.”

“The man?”

“He’s dead.”

Hayley noticed that Tommy Welling was clutching his mother and sobbing hard. The aftermath of the attack bore down on them all. Tears welled up in Hayley’s eyes as shock, bewilderment and maybe disbelief set in. Before Jess could say anything the radio on the dead guy crackled, Ken picked it up, and they heard one of them trying to get in contact. “Come in, Raymond. You there?”

Ken looked at Jess. “They’ll be back soon. You should go.”

Jess nodded and scooped up the M4 and stepped out into the hallway, casting a glance to the east and west. Before setting their plan in motion, it was agreed that Jess and Hayley would leave and Clara who was the teacher and knew where the tunnel passage was to the school would take them down and go with them. What they hadn’t banked on was Tommy choosing to go.

"I'm coming with you," he said wiping tears from his eyes.

"No, you should stay here," Jess said.

"There's nothing left for me," he replied looking back at his dead mother.

"And your father?"

"Absent."

She nodded.

Tommy walked across the room and stood by the doorway ready to leave. Jess didn't know him well enough to argue, and it didn't look as if anyone else in the room was going to convince him otherwise. He sniffed hard, holding back his tears, and pawed at his eyes.

"Okay."

Ken kept the other gun from the fallen man and the plan was they would barricade themselves inside the homeowners lounge and if anyone tried to get through the door, he would fire at them. It wasn't exactly an airtight plan but it beat trying to get all seventy-odd people out of the building. That would have likely ended in a massacre.

Jess clutched her daughter's hand and Clara led the way, ushering Tommy on towards the elevators. Clara tapped the button several times, and they stepped back. There were two elevators in front of them, one on the left and the other on the right. On the left above the elevator doors they could see one was in use and based on the numbers lighting up, the elevator was climbing. Clara tapped the button again, nervous at the thought of another deadly confrontation. Jess clutched the gun aiming at the right elevator while they waited for it to make it up three floors.

She fully expected it to open and be full of armed men but when the right one dinged and the doors slid open, it was empty. They hurried inside fully aware that the left elevator was close to arriving on the fifteenth floor. Clara tapped the button to get the doors to close just as they heard the ding of the left elevator arriving.

The doors sealed out the sound of men talking as they got off.

Jess's heart was pounding in her chest as the elevator made its descent into the unknown.

Chapter 16

Initially, things didn't seem out of the ordinary. Cayden assumed Raymond and Ty were in the homeowners lounge with the residents except when they tried to open the door, it wouldn't budge. Vic rattled the knob, then gave it a shove but it wouldn't open.

"Raymond?" Cayden shouted. There was no reply. He turned to Vic and told him to check the stairwell just in case they'd stepped away. Vic nodded and took off in that direction. He hadn't made it a few feet when he stopped and called back.

"Ty?" He darted into the apartment next door to the lounge and the rest of them followed. Cayden went berserk when he saw Ty's body on the ground in a pool of blood. Charging back to the lounge he banged on the door.

"Open up."

He stepped back and fired a flurry of rounds at the

area around the door handle, sparks flew and he thought that would be enough. He didn't expect what happened next. Rounds from the other side lanced the door, and one of them skimmed his arm. All the men hit the ground as the wall behind them was peppered in a sweeping fashion from left to right.

Cayden looked over to Leon. He could tell he wanted to rub it in and say that he'd warned him but he was in no mood to be raked over the coals for something he thought was under control. Vic tried to get Raymond on the radio again as until they got confirmation that he was dead they assumed he was still alive.

"How the hell did this happen?" Vic shouted as more rounds continued. Then it went silent.

"Come in, Raymond."

"Raymond's dead," a male voice said coming over the radio. "Both of your men are and if you don't get the hell out of here, you'll join them."

Cayden motioned to Vic to slide over the radio. He tossed it and it landed a few feet from him. He crawled on his belly and grabbed it up. Cayden pressed the button and spoke into the radio. "Who am I speaking with?"

"Ken Rogers."

"Well Ken, you have just made one big mistake."

"Really? Because the way it looks to me, you're the ones who fucked up."

Cayden was fuming. As soon as he got inside, he was going to take great pleasure in killing him. He gritted his teeth. "I'm gonna make this pretty simple. Open the door and there's a chance you'll live."

"A chance? Huh!" Ken scoffed. "How generous of you. I think I'll take my chances on this side."

Cayden sneered and squeezed the radio hard. This whole thing was getting away from him. They were down three men and now there were only seven of them left. Cayden got up and while staying low moved away from the apartment. He needed to think. He needed a pick-me-up. Something to even him out. He made it to the far end of the hallway and pulled out a baggie of coke. Leon came up from behind him, still looking over his shoulder while Vic remained in place just in case anyone attempted to open the door.

"What are you doing?" Leon asked.

"Thinking."

"Haven't you had enough of that shit?"

"What are you, my mother?"

"Can't you see it's clouding your judgment?"

"I swear, Leon, you might be my friend but if you say that one more time I'm going to drop you."

He tapped out some coke onto the back of his hand and snorted it, his eyes rolled back in his head and he felt the rush as it hit his system.

"We've lost three people. How many more have to die before you wake the hell up? We need to leave and now."

Cayden whirled around. "You know, Leon, you were always a pussy. Why I have let you drag me down is a mystery. I should have got rid of you a long time ago."

"The only reason you are alive is because of me. How many times have I saved your ass? If it wasn't for me you would be rotting in a jail cell by now so you want to drop me, go ahead and see where you end up."

Cayden shook his head and looked past him. He got back on the radio. "Hank, come in."

Hank, Pat, Jimmy and Jerome were on the lower floors still performing a search for the drugs and making sure that no one got in or out of the building.

"Go ahead," Hank said.

"Found anything yet?"

"Nothing so far. Are you on the sixth floor?" Hank asked.

"No, the fifteenth, why?"

"I saw the elevator stopped on the seventh, then it continued on to the sixth."

"Get up there now! Block both sides of the stairwell and have one of you watch the elevator. It looks like some of our guests have got out."

* * *

Alex heard the message over the radio. After hearing the gunfire, he'd headed down from the roof to the ninth floor, which appeared to be empty. He was in the process of figuring out how to draw the men away from the fifteenth floor when he saw the elevator going down and then heard Cayden's message.

He hurried along to the stairwell and jogged down three flights of steps to the sixth floor and darted into one of the apartments. He was keeping a close eye on the hallway through a crack in the door when the elevator dinged.

* * *

Jess's heart was racing as she exited the elevator heading for the stairwell. She kept a firm grip on Hayley's hand as Clara led the way. She was completely unaware of the approaching threat because Ken was the only one who had a radio. They had just made it past room 6008 when she felt a hand clasp around her mouth and drag her backwards. Hayley let out a scream and then it ended when she saw who it was — Alex.

* * *

"Dad?"

"Get in now," he said.

Clara, Tommy and Hayley ducked into the room and Alex closed the door. He released his grip on Jess's mouth and she hugged him tight. He ran a hand over Hayley's face and gave her a kiss on the forehead. That's when he noticed the dried blood.

"What the hell?"

"It's okay, I'm not hurt," she said.

"Where are the others?"

"Still in the homeowners lounge. They're safe. They have a rifle and have locked themselves in. Two of their men are dead," Jess said.

"How many are there?" Alex asked.

"Ten. At least there were ten."

"So seven left because I killed one. Listen, they have locked the exits with padlocks. Now we might be able to get out if I shoot the lock but there are men coming right now."

The radio crackled, and he heard them come over the speaker. "Cayden, we're on the sixth now. No one is here."

"Check the apartments," Cayden replied.

"Shit!" Alex muttered pulling back from the door. They had few options. Stay in the room and attack when the two guys entered, or try and make a break for the stairwell while they were in one of the apartments. He paced back and forth for a second or two.

"Dad? What do we do?" Hayley asked.

"Look, I'm going to distract them, draw them away to the east stairwell. Once I'm in there, I want you to head to the west."

"No, Alex, we just found you."

He wrapped a hand around her neck and pulled Jess in close to him. "I'll meet you in the basement."

"We can fight." She lifted the gun.

"It's too dangerous."

"But—"

"Jess, just listen to me. Wait here, keep the door cracked ever so slightly. Once I'm in the stairwell make a break for it."

She shook her head but there was no more time to

wait. He could hear the men getting nearer. There was one coming from the east, and another from the west. They were going apartment to apartment checking, occasionally firing their weapons. Alex got close to the door and peered out. He had to time it just right. One mistake and it was over. He watched as they exited one apartment and darted into the next. He looked the other way, another guy did the same. This was it. Alex looked back at Jess, smiled then darted out. He raced down the hallway and was within spitting distance of the stairwell when one of the men came out. Alex slammed into him, knocking him flying back. Alex lost his footing and tumbled but without wasting a second he was up and running. Instead of trying to reach the stairwell he darted into the elevator. His shoulder collided with the back as gunfire unleashed. He smashed one button trying to get the doors to close, then hit the one for the tenth floor. The doors slipped closed just as one of the men reached the elevator. He heard them bang on the outside as it started to go up.

Over the radio he heard, "He's heading up."

The odds of getting out were stacked against him. He just needed to delay things. He waited until he was around the eighth floor before he hit the red stop button used by maintenance. Having it stop there would throw them off. The elevator jerked for a second and he looked above him and used the butt of the rifle to lift up one of the tiles, then using the handles inside the elevator he launched himself up and climbed over the lip into the elevator shaft. Before replacing the tile he leaned down and used the tip of the M4 to extend his reach and touch the button to get the elevator going again. It lurched up and began to climb. He closed the top and hung on for dear life as he continued up to the tenth floor.

As soon as it arrived, and the doors slid open, a flurry of rounds filled the elevator shattering the mirrors that wrapped around the inside.

"Where is he?" one of the men said stepping into the elevator. The guy looked up and through the thin air holes Alex could just make out the top of his head. He had his gun on the ready just in case but thankfully he didn't have to use it. The man exited.

"It stopped on the eighth floor, you idiot. Let's go."

He breathed a sigh of relief and hoped to God that Jess and the others had managed to escape.

* * *

Minutes earlier, Jess stood by the door and saw the horrifying scene play out before her. She was tempted to engage but once she saw Alex reach the elevator, she knew he was safe. Both armed men entered the east stairwell. The second they disappeared, she motioned to the other three to head out. She pushed the door open and told them to run to the west stairwell. As they bolted, Hayley slipped and landed on her knees. Jess scooped an arm under hers and they forged forward. As soon as they were inside, they began to make their way down. The stairwell was quiet. Jess peered over the bannister to make sure there was no one farther down. She looked up and couldn't hear or see anyone.

"It shouldn't take us long," Clara said.

Tommy looked despondent and kept close to Clara as she led the way. Jess kept turning and looking up expecting at any second to hear one of the men return but they didn't. They made it down to the second floor and were just about to go down one more flight of steps when the door opened on the first floor.

"Hank!" a voice yelled out before several rounds were fired. Jess slipped back, telling the others to get down as they scrambled to escape the ricochet of bullets. She raised the M4 and whirled it over the bannister to return fire. Each time she did, she motioned to the others to move down. If they didn't press on and get out of that stairwell they would become trapped from above and below.

The guy at the door didn't let up. He would unload, pull back, the door would swing closed but before it sealed, he would push it open and fire again. However, because she was returning fire, he wouldn't stick his face out so he was shooting haphazardly trying to keep them under a constant hail of bullets.

Jess pressed her back to the wall and threw up a hand to tell them to wait. She pressed forward, taking a huge risk that one of the bullets wouldn't hit her. She saw the barrel stick out of the door and waited for him to finish unloading a few rounds before she kicked the door that was closing wide and came around and lanced his chest with two rounds. The look of shock on his face would stay with her forever. She would have grabbed up his rifle but at the far end of the hall she saw another man running forward, raising his rifle. She opened fire then shouted to Hayley and the others to move their asses.

They hurried down past her heading for the basement.

Once they were in the clear she slammed the door closed and hurried down the steps after them. She knew they only had a few seconds before the next guy would be on their case. The closer they got to the basement, the slower Clara became.

Lights flickered and the sound of something groaning could be heard coming up from the basement. Within seconds the lights went out, and they were shrouded in darkness.

"Shit!"

"Mom!" Hayley cried.

"It's okay, I'm here," Jess replied. "Keep going." She wasn't even looking at them when she called out but then she saw why they were hesitant to continue. Most of the basement was underwater. The last ten steps were covered. Clara bent down and touched it.

"It's freezing cold."

Jess kept looking back and forth. She heard the door open on the first floor.

"Mom?" Hayley said looking back at her. "What now?"

A hundred thoughts went through her mind in those seconds. Would the guy shoot them on sight? If they entered the water would they drown? She couldn't lose her daughter! Where was Alex? And even if they escaped would they freeze to death from being soaked?

"I'll go," Tommy said.

"But the door is locked at the far end," Jess replied.

"Then give me the rifle."

"No."

Suddenly gunfire erupted. Jess returned fire and then pulled back and they all moved closer to the water.

"Decide now what we are doing or we are all going to die!" Tommy yelled. Before he got his answer, he decided for himself. "Ah screw this, I'm going." He launched himself off the steps into chest-high waters and disappeared below.

Clara yelled out his name. "Tommy!"

Clara waded into the water to find him but Tommy resurfaced. There was still enough room to stay above the water and breathe but they would have to move fast. Jess called out to Clara. "Here, take this."

She tossed the rifle to her and then told Hayley to go with Clara.

"Mom?"

More gunfire erupted.

"I'm not leaving you here."

"You need to get out. I will be okay."

"Mom."

"Clara, please, take her."

Hayley tried to resist but Clara pulled her into the water and Tommy assisted. Jess watched them disappear behind a wall, heading down into the tunnel's passage. Then she raised her hands above her head and locked her fingers. She knew that if she waded into the water the chances of all of them escaping would be slim. If she could hold off the other guy, they might just have a chance. "I don't have a weapon," she shouted out to him, getting down onto her knees as a sign of surrender. She looked up and saw a barrel-chested man come around the corner. A light shone from the end of his M4 lighting up her face. He looked past her.

"Where are the others?" he demanded.

"Gone." He gritted his teeth, came down the flight of steps not convinced. He looked over and saw nothing but water lapping against the wall. He turned back to Jess and with the back of his gun, struck her in the head, knocking her unconscious.

Chapter 17

After gathering a couple of shotguns, additional ammo, a hammer, thermal blankets, a couple more ballistic vests to replace the ones that had been soaked, and some diving gear, Solomon and the others had taken the boat over to the school. He'd already slipped into a wet suit that they kept on hand for any water incidents. It would keep his body protected from the cold. The problem was they could only find one. With the power out in the public safety building they were lucky to find even that. It was now early evening, and even darker outside.

"I gotta tell you, chief, this is the strangest weather we have ever had. Ain't nothing normal about this," Scott said. "My old man used to talk about a time when Mother Nature would take back the planet. I'm thinking he was right."

"It's just another storm. A bad one, but that's all. Give

it a day, it will be gone," Lucas said as Solomon brought the boat around to the main doors of the school. Water had already flooded in.

Scott shook his head. "Yeah right. You ever seen it like this?"

"Happened back in the '60s," Lucas replied.

"But that was an earthquake. There were no reports of one and I never felt anything."

"Guys, shut the hell up and give me a hand," Solomon said as he cut the engine and used a hammer to smash out the thick glass in the front windows of the school. "Keep the boat steady."

Lucas looked concerned. "I'm telling you, chief, this is not a good idea."

"You have a better one?"

"Yeah, get the hell out," Lucas said. "We head back to Anchorage, get SWAT and come back."

"It's an hour on a good day. This is a not a good day. I'm not leaving those people in there."

"And how do you expect to get them out? This boat

doesn't hold more than five or six people."

"While I go in, I want you and Scott to go find another boat."

Scott looked concerned. "Chief, you're gonna need us."

"I know. That's why you're getting the boat."

"No. I meant inside."

"Then you better find a boat fast," he said.

"How about we get one now and then you don't go in alone?" Lucas said. "Makes sense, right?"

"Time is against us. Hold the boat steady," Solomon said stepping out and through the window, dropping down into the water. The cold gripped him hard and reminded him of how brutal winters in Alaska could be.

"You can't be in there long," Lucas said. "I don't want to end up finding your body floating around. I'm not burying you."

"Don't worry about me, just go get that boat." He reached for the scuba gear and slid his arms into the straps, hoisting the oxygen canister higher up on his back.

Scott passed over a shotgun, and he turned on a headlamp. A long yellow beam shot out illuminating the inside of the school.

“Okay, hurry up,” he said before venturing into the bowels of the school. Books, papers and chairs floated on the surface of the water. It was eerily quiet inside, only the sound of water sloshing against the wall, and pouring down into the basement.

* * *

In the underground tunnel that came out at the school, Clara held the M4 above her head and waded through another yard of darkness. It was pitch-black down there and freezing cold. If she hadn’t walked that tunnel every day for the past four years, and hadn’t known how many steps it took to reach the end, she might have panicked. Instead, she tried to remain optimistic if only for the sake of Tommy and Hayley.

“How much further?” Hayley asked.

“We’re getting close.”

“You know I can carry the gun,” Tommy said.

"It's okay."

"I mean if it's getting heavy."

Clara was concerned for his mental state. Losing a mother under normal circumstances was hard enough but seeing his mother shot to death — that was going to screw him up badly. In the silence she thought back to those final seconds as Jess lured the second gunman in, telling him that someone was hurt and bleeding out. Four of them had jumped the guy, one of those was Tommy's mother. The gun went off, they managed to get him down and Ken wrestled the gun away and shot him. For a brief second they felt a sense of justice, victory, even hope but that all ended when they stepped back and saw Mary-Anne clutching her stomach.

Slowly but surely they made their way to the far end of the tunnel and arrived at the double doors. The glass was already partly split. She ran her fingers over it. Tommy grabbed the chain and lifted it above the water's surface. "She was right."

"Stand back," Clara said. She put her arm back to keep

them away. She'd never fired a gun in her life. She glanced at it and did what anyone would and just squeezed the trigger and hoped for the best. Four rounds disappeared below the water. She moved in and lifted it. Nothing. It hadn't made one damn change.

"Let me try," Tommy said.

"You're a kid. I'm not letting you use this."

"How about using this?" Haley waded through the water and pulled off a fire extinguisher that was hanging on a hook in the tunnel. She brought it back and told Tommy to lift the chain but move to one side so he didn't get hit. She raised up the extinguisher and brought it down hard against the padlock. The steel collided but nothing happened. Clara even stepped in to have a go but that didn't work.

"Shit!" Clara yelled. She stared back down the tunnel. All three of them were shivering like mad. The water was so cold she couldn't feel her feet, and her legs had gone numb. As frustration set in so did desperation.

"Stand back." Clara took aim and opened fire on the

window. The glass cracked ever so slightly. With her hope renewed she went to fire again, but it just clicked. She squeezed again. "Oh come on!" It was out of bullets.

Clara waded forward, turned the rifle over and started hammering on the window in frustration. "Tommy, give me a hand."

Tommy took the extinguisher from Hayley and joined her. They pounded that window causing even more fissures to appear, spreading outward. "What kind of windows did they install in this?" Tommy asked.

As they continued pounding, a small light appeared in the dark. It was facing them on the other side. "What's that?" Hayley asked.

Clara squinted and for a brief second she thought it was the men. She told them to get back into the tunnel. But as the light got bigger, and the person got closer to the door, she suddenly recognized who it was.

"Chief?"

She waded to the door and banged on it. "Chief!"

They returned to hammering on the one side while the

chief worked the other with a hammer. Within seconds the glass shattered, and an opening appeared. "God, am I glad to see you," Clara said. They spent the next few minutes carefully climbing up and through into the school. On the other side it wasn't much better. The water was still as high as ever. Solomon led them back through the basement, and up the stairs. They climbed up onto the counters that wrapped around the side of the building so they could get out of the water.

"Where are the others?" Solomon asked.

"They have them," Clara replied. "They're all on the fifteenth floor. There are seven men remaining."

"And Alex?"

"Alive. At least the last time we saw him enter the elevator."

"Any of you hurt?"

"Just cold," she said. All three of them sat on a counter and shivered hard.

"There's a boat coming. Should be here in a minute. Two of my officers will take you out of here." He turned to head back in.

"Chief. You're going in?"

He nodded.

"But..."

"It's all right," he said. "Just stay here, you'll be safe."

"If we don't freeze to death," Tommy replied, cupping his hands and blowing into them.

* * *

"We lost them!" Jimmy said over the radio. Cayden had just about enough of this shit. Fuming, he motioned to Vic and Leon to follow him and he headed over to the lounge and told them to unload multiple rounds through the door. He didn't intend to get the door opened, he just wanted to kill a few people. On the other side they heard screams and groaning. He smiled, feeling some sense of control even if nothing had changed. Once they were done, they backed away, and he got on the radio again.

"Ken, you still alive?" he asked.

There was a long pause before he got a response. "You asshole."

He laughed. "Good to hear your voice. For a second there I thought I might have lost you." He released the button and waited for a reply.

"You just killed two kids, and a mother," Ken replied. Leon looked at Cayden and he knew what he was thinking.

"Yeah, well don't say I didn't warn you. You wanted to go play the big fucking hero and look where it's got you. Their blood is on your hands," Cayden said before releasing the button. Ken didn't reply.

"Open the door, Ken, and you have my word no one else will be harmed."

"Bullshit."

Cayden turned to Vic and in a low voice he said, "For someone so pissed, strange he hasn't fired back, right?"

"He's out," Vic replied.

Cayden nodded, stepped forward and fired again at the door riddling it with holes, then stepped back and kicked the door hard. The lock broke away from the frame and now he could just make out the people inside, beyond a mountain of tables and chairs they'd stacked behind the door. "Ken, you have until the count of ten to move this shit out of the way or we are going to open fire and kill more people. Now you decide what matters more!"

He couldn't see him beyond the door as it was only cracked open a bit, but he heard him tell the others to pull the chairs and tables away. Cayden glanced at Vic and smiled. "See, they just needed a little motivation." His gaze bounced to Leon who didn't look happy. It didn't take them long to remove the barricade. Once the door was open, Cayden walked in with a hop in his step. He glanced around the room, looked down at Raymond dead on the ground and tutted. "People, people. Why don't you listen? No one had harmed you, but then you go and do this. Now who killed my men?"

No one said anything. They backed up against the window, cowering before him.

"Okay. Ken? Which one of you is Ken?"

An older guy stepped forward. Cayden walked over to him and swung his rifle around his back and placed a hand on his neck. He led him into the center of the room. "Oh Ken. Let me guess, this was your grand idea. What did you hope to achieve, huh?" Cayden looked around at the others.

"Please. We just want to leave."

"You want to leave?"

He nodded.

"Okay. You can leave."

Ken looked back at him, unconvinced.

"No seriously. You can leave. Go. There's the door."

Ken took a few steps and kept his eyes on Cayden.

"Vic, move out of the way. Our guest here wants to leave."

Vic and Leon entered the room and stepped to one side. Ken shuffled towards the door, certain that Cayden was going to shoot him in the back. Cayden watched in amusement as Ken exited the room, then broke into a run. Cayden looked at Leon for a second then pulled his Beretta from the holster, walked casually over to the door and fired one round hitting him in the back. He turned back to the rest of the people who were crying and cowering. "I said he could leave. Just didn't say it was alive."

* * *

Alex dropped down into the elevator and exited on the tenth floor, he hurried to the opposite stairwell that the men had gone to and started making his way down. Relieved that he wasn't going to have to start negotiating for the lives of those inside, he couldn't help wonder if they were truly safe. Jess had said they had barricaded themselves in and maybe that would hold for a while and perhaps Cayden would walk away, but if he thought for a second that one of them knew where his drugs were, he wouldn't stop until he was in. Alex stopped on the third floor and brought the radio up to his lips. He hesitated and then pressed the button.

"Cayden," Alex said.

There was static, then a voice on the line.

"Who's this?"

"The guy who has what you want. Now I'm all for fun

and games but you're really grinding on my last nerve, so listen up, I'm sure you want to get the hell out of here as much as I do so here's how this is going to work. I have divided up your little stash into four different places in the building. Without my assistance you will never find them. Now I will give you the location of each one but not until the residents are safe and away from here."

"Safe? They are free to go anytime they like. In fact I just let one leave."

Alex's brow furrowed. He knew he was bullshitting.

"Funny, I heard they were barricaded inside the lounge."

"Yeah, that didn't exactly work out well for them."

Alex chewed over his response.

"Look, I don't give a fuck, like I said, I have what you want. So let's reach an agreement, shall we?"

"Who are you?" Cayden asked.

"The agreement."

"I don't make deals with those I don't know. You could be bluffing."

He waited for a second. Jess and Hayley were safe, so it didn't matter if he knew his name. "Alex Riley."

"Officer Alex Riley." He heard him chuckle on the other end of the line. "So what do you have in mind, officer?"

"I want all your men out of here. Once I have everyone to safety, I will give you the locations of the drugs."

He snorted. "And why should I believe you?"

"Look, I can quite easily dump this shit out the window and let Mother Nature take a hit or you can stop jerking me off and do as I say…"

"Um, let me think about that." There was a long pause. "Tempting but no… there's been a change of plans."

"Yeah, how's that?"

Alex heard him chuckle. "Because I have your wife."

Chapter 18

Even with the wet suit on, the water was freezing cold. Minutes earlier Solomon waded through the tunnel, the headlamp illuminating the way. He held his shotgun and Glock above his head, and had stashed additional ammo in a bag that was tied over his shoulder and hoisted high on his back to prevent water getting in.

His mind flashed back to his last argument with Natalie before she left him. Back then he'd been so stubborn. He drank hard, worked harder and what little time he had to himself, he just wanted to be left alone. It wasn't exactly the best conditions for a marriage, and it was very different to when they first met. Back then he was young, and utterly smitten by her dark hair, and green eyes. Somewhere along the way he'd lost sight of her, and what life was really about.

Solomon continued on down the narrow passage, guilt and regret washing over him. Had he listened to her they could have had a life in Anchorage away from here, away from the very things that tore them apart.

It was times like these when he saw how fragile life was, and how quickly everything could change, that he realized what was important. It wasn't like Natalie didn't mean anything to him. He loved her dearly. But that had only become clearer after she packed her bags and drove away.

Coming home was never the same after that.

It was easier to knock off work and spend the few remaining hours he had in the day down at the Anchor Inn, then sleep the rest of the time.

"I swear, if I make it through this situation I will turn things around," he said out loud, as if anyone could hear him. Solomon finally made it to the bottom of the stairs and water poured off him as he climbed to the first floor. He took a few seconds to put his Glock into the holster and then peered down the corridor. It was quiet. Not a sound. He was about to enter when he heard a voice above.

* * *

Alex paced back and forth. Was he bluffing? Had they not managed to get out? Where was Hayley? He got back on the radio and called him on it. “Bullshit! Put her on.”

The radio went silent and the next voice that came on made his stomach sink.

“Alex?”

“Jess.”

“There’s six of them left,” she screamed before Cayden got back on the radio.

“I’ll give you this, you certainly picked a feisty woman. Do you know she killed two of my men?”

“You lay one hand on her and I will—”

“You will do nothing! Now I’m done playing games. You have thirty minutes to bring what is mine to the fifteenth floor, or I will personally toss your wife off the top of this building.”

“Cayden!” Alex shouted.

“Tick tock.”

The radio went dead. Fear shot through Alex. He tried

again to get through to him but he wouldn't respond. He swallowed hard and was about to race up to the seventh floor when he heard steps behind him. Alex spun around to find Solomon.

"Sounds like you've got yourself into quite the predicament."

"Solomon? But I thought you were dead."

"Unfortunately I'm not that lucky."

He was soaked and wearing a wet suit but had his duty belt around him, a bag over his shoulder and a shotgun in hand.

"Please tell me there are more of you?"

"I'm afraid this is it, but there is an upside. Your daughter is safe."

"Hayley?"

"She's over at the school with two others. Black and Parker will take care of them."

Although he was relieved to hear that his daughter was out of harm's way that didn't take away the fear he had over losing Jess.

"You want to bring me up to speed on what's going on?" Solomon said leaning against the wall out of breath. Alex spent the next minute or so relaying information as he climbed the stairwell up to the seventh floor to collect the first batch of drugs. He wasn't sure what he would do next but he wasn't going to take chances, not after seeing so many killed already. When they made it into the apartment and he brought a chair over to retrieve the drugs, Solomon continued, "You're just going to hand it over?"

"That's not exactly what I had in mind but what do you expect me to do?"

"You hand over that and she's as good as dead, you know that, right?"

Alex nodded and dropped down off the chair with one of the bags full of heroin. "And that's why I'm not handing it over until she's safe." He paused to take a breath. "Besides, what other options do we have?"

"You let me take the drugs," Solomon said.

"What?"

"I'll say that I stashed them in the apartment and I wasn't going to let you hand them over."

"I don't see how that helps."

"I'll say I killed you."

Alex laughed, looking back at him. "Are you serious?"

"Danny, and Greg are dead. They know that. They've killed people to get those drugs. It's not a far stretch of the imagination to assume that I wouldn't do the same. They've dealt with dirty cops."

He shook his head and walked out of the apartment heading for the ninth floor. "They won't buy it, Solomon, and besides, that doesn't help Jess. In fact it's likely to get her killed and the rest of the residents. You want that on your conscience?"

They ascended the steps two at a time, hurrying to meet the deadline. Alex knew what Solomon was trying to do. It was human nature to try and come up with some harebrained idea but realistically there was no easy way out. The best he could do was to hand over a portion of the drugs as a sign of good faith, and offer the rest in exchange for her. As ludicrous as it sounded that was the only option they had. Every other way ended with Jess dead.

"Okay, so here's what we'll do. I'll head up the east stairwell. You go to the west. I'll hand over the bag and tell them they get the rest if Jess goes with me. The only thing they want are these drugs, so the chances are they aren't going to stay up there with the residents. You can get the residents out via the west stairwell, I'll handle the rest from there."

"Are you insane?" Solomon said.

"About my wife? Yeah."

Solomon shook his head. "You know he'll kill you or her the moment you try to walk."

Alex didn't respond so Solomon grabbed a hold of him. "Alex. Stop. Are you listening to me?"

"I know the risks," Alex yelled back in his face.

"No you don't. This idea is absurd."

"And yours wasn't? C'mon, man!"

"I've been doing this job a long time and what I'm

trying to do is help you."

"Bullshit. You are trying to get yourself killed. The question is why?"

Solomon stopped climbing the stairs. "You think I want to die?"

"If Kip was telling the truth, you sure as hell didn't want to live."

He studied him. "Fine. You do it your way but this is on your head."

"You didn't let me finish, did you?" Alex said. "Of course I know he will come after me. Of course I know he's liable to try and shoot Jess in the back as she walks away, that's why I had an ace up my sleeve."

"Which is?"

"Down in the basement are containers full of gasoline, and a shitload of empty jars, courtesy of our friend Kip. Once we have gathered together what we need, I'll show you what I had in mind."

Solomon gave him a skeptical look but refrained from questioning any further. They hurried around on the ninth floor to two apartments and one more on the tenth, zipped up the duffel bag and hauled it down to the basement. When they made it to the bottom, Alex looked at his watch. They still had another quarter of an hour left to go.

"Alex. Would you tell me what is going on?"

"You're going to need to do this," Alex said.

"Me?"

"You're wearing the wet suit. You're going to see two generators. Nearby should be four army-style metal canisters. That's the gasoline. Bring one of those back. You'll also find some mason jars on a shelf if they're not already underwater in the storage area. We're gonna need those."

Solomon flipped on the headlamp, hooked on the oxygen tank he'd left at the foot of the stairwell and waded down into the water. "This is nuts." There was about thirty inches between the surface of the water and the top of the ceiling in the basement. It was continuing to rise.

"Get in. Get out."

"Don't worry. I plan on it."

He swam off and disappeared below the depths. Alex fumbled around in his pockets for cigarettes. He put one between his lips, lit it and inhaled deeply allowing the nicotine to calm his nerves. There was no guarantee that what he had in mind would work. The odds were stacked against them. He knew that. But he wasn't going to leave Jess there. No way in hell.

As he stood there waiting, he thought back to his conversation with his wife on the day Ethan died. The heartbreaking message had come in the middle of the night. Shaken awake by his superior, he was told he had an urgent call. He figured Jess was having another breakdown, trying to cope with him being away from home. She'd called him numerous times, and he'd managed to calm her down but this time it wasn't her on the other end of the phone. It was her father. He was clear and straight to the point.

"You need to come home, Alex."

"What's going on?"

"Ethan has taken a turn for the worst. He's real sick."

"How sick?" Alex replied.

"Doctors don't think he's going to make it."

Now he'd seen all manner of horrors in the Middle East, and watched many of his best friends get killed, but nothing came close to receiving that news. There wasn't much about the rest of that phone call that he recalled. It was like his world imploded.

"The family is with Jess but she needs you here."

"I'll do my best."

The military came to his aid and rushed him out of there and within hours he was on a plane home, but by the time he arrived it was too late. He didn't know until he stepped on the tarmac and was greeted by her father.

Not getting to say goodbye to his kid destroyed him.

He didn't think he could feel as much anguish as he did in the days after. Even though their families rallied around, cooked meals, and were there for them, nothing could have prepared them for what would happen after they left. Eventually everyone had to return home, go back to their jobs and life had to continue. Picking up the pieces, trying to summon the strength to get through another day — that was the hardest part. There were days when he didn't want to get out of bed, he didn't want to put on a brave front for his daughter, for his wife or anyone. The truth was he wanted to die. The pain was too much.

Alex sat there quietly thinking of the past when there was a huge splash off to his right and Solomon emerged like a Navy SEAL trudging out of the sea onto dry land. In one hand he carried a large green canister that was sealed at the top, and in the other a bag full of mason jars clinking together.

He yanked the respirator away from his mouth and took a deep breath.

"Holy cow it's cold. I don't know how we are going to get people out of here. There's no way they are going to withstand that temperature."

"Well, first things first we have to get people out,"

Alex said scooping up the canister and bag and going up to the next level to begin putting into motion what he had in mind. He took out twelve mason jars, unscrewed the caps and poured in gasoline, filling each one before sealing them tight.

"What are you doing?" Solomon asked as Alex worked in silence.

Once he had them filled, he emptied out the duffel bag of heroin and filled it up with the jars. Then he covered them and squeezed them together using the bricks of heroin. Once they were completely covered, he took the canister of gasoline and drenched the bag in the flammable liquid, then lifted it a few times and jiggled it around to see if the glass would clatter. It didn't. He'd packed the heroin so tight around the jars there was no room for them to move. Then he zipped up the bag, leaving two of the mason jars out. He went over to one of the dead men laying on the ground in the hallway and ripped off a scrap of his shirt. He took out his knife and cut a slit in the metal mason jar top and threaded the cloth through it before screwing the top on. He then doused it with more gasoline so it was truly covered. Next he handed it to Solomon. "You got a lighter?"

"No."

He went over to the dead guy and fished through his pockets. There was nothing. "Shit." He had one but he needed it. Alex glanced at his watch, he had just over five minutes before Cayden would be expecting him. He dashed into one of the apartments and used his flashlight to search around for a lighter. He didn't find one, but he found matches. He tossed them to Solomon and then told him what to do.

"Well if this goes well, I guess I'll see you outside."

Solomon nodded. "And if doesn't..."

"I'll see you on the other side."

"One hell of a first day on the job, huh?" Solomon asked.

"Beats working a desk job."

There was a chance they wouldn't see each other again, but that was the risk that came with the job. He scooped up the bag and gave Solomon a slap on the back before heading off up the east stairwell.

Chapter 19

Cayden sat in a chair with his boots up on a table and a smug look on his face as if he had somehow proved his point. Leon glanced at his watch, stared down the hallway to the stairwell, then back towards the elevator. Hank was watching to see if Officer Riley would be coming up that way. He shook his head to indicate no one was coming.

Leon stepped back into the room and walked over to Cayden.

"A moment of your time."

"What is it now, Leon?"

He cast a glance over his shoulder at the residents huddled together.

"In private."

Cayden groaned and swung his legs off the table. He led him out down the hallway to another apartment so they were out of earshot.

"What do you want?" Cayden asked.

"What are you going to do with the residents once you have the stash?"

He shrugged. "What do you think I'm gonna do?"

Leon stared back with a look of disbelief. He didn't need to spell it out, he knew.

"There are women and children among that group."

"And they've seen our faces," Cayden said.

"So you're just going to execute them."

"I'm not."

"Of course not. You wouldn't want that on your conscience."

"What is your problem?"

Leon shook his head. "I didn't sign up for this."

Cayden cocked his head. "Okay, hold on a second, what happened to you, Leon? You used to have a spine." He paused. "It's her, isn't it? Julie." He tapped his temple with his index finger. "I've seen the way she's infected your mind. I'm right, aren't I?"

He wasn't wrong. Since meeting Julie in a café in Anchorage, a woman who wasn't part of their world but soon became his wife and eventually the mother of his child, he'd changed. Julie would say the change was for the better, Cayden would say for the worse. The fact was that growing up in a life of crime Leon knew no better, he didn't see the other side of the coin until he met her. Those he ran with, including the woman he'd slept with up until a few years ago, only cared about one thing — money. Julie wasn't like that. She wasn't pushy, she had a way of helping him see that he wasn't just damaging lives through violence but destroying his own.

"You're just jealous."

"Jealous? Please," Cayden said pulling out a cigarette and lighting it.

"Your wife took your kid and walked out. Now you hate the fact that I'm moving on, and that I want to get out of this."

"Get out?" He turned around with a scowl on his face. He blew out smoke.

"Cayden, we are not teenagers anymore. We don't have to prove a point. I want to be around to see my kid grow up. I'm gonna be in his life."

"I'm gonna be in mine."

"Really? When was the last time you dropped by her house?"

"Screw you, Leon," Cayden said. "I don't need to listen to this shit."

He turned to walk out.

"After this I'm done. I'm out."

Cayden turned and smiled. "You're never out. You know that."

"I'm serious. I'm done. And as for those people in there. You want them dead, kill them yourself."

Leon brushed past him and headed out into the hallway. He was on his way towards the west stairwell back to the homeowners lounge when Vic yelled for Cayden. Leon twisted around and saw an officer standing in the doorway of the east stairwell.

* * *

Carrying the bag in one hand, and the M4 in the other, Alex took in the sight of three armed assailants.

Within a matter of seconds, two more appeared coming out of the lounge and walked halfway down the hallway before the sixth emerged, locking eyes with him. He smiled, and Alex had a feeling that was Cayden.

"Officer Riley. Glad to see you made the smart decision." Cayden glanced at his watch. "I was just on my way to get your lovely wife and toss her off the roof. Pity."

"Where is she?" Alex asked, remaining where he was. He was ready to return fire and duck out if they tried anything.

"All in good time. Is that my package?" Cayden asked making his way down.

"Don't come any further," Alex said making a motion with his rifle. Cayden was clutching a handgun, it was down at his side. He turned to one of his men and whispered something and they jogged back to the homeowners lounge.

"I want to see it," Cayden demanded.

"Once I see my wife."

"A family man. I like that. You know, Officer Riley… or can I call you Alex?" Alex didn't respond so Cayden continued. "I respect a man who's willing to risk his life for his own. But I got to ask you, where did you find it?"

"Does it matter?"

"No, just curious."

Right then Jess emerged from the homeowners lounge being shoved forward by one of Cayden's guys.

"Alex!" she yelled and was about to run towards him when Cayden grabbed a hold of her and brought his handgun up to her side.

"Now slide over what's mine."

"That's not how this works," Alex said lowering the bag to the ground. He kept his rifle trained on Cayden as he reached into his pocket and pulled out one of the bricks of heroin. He tossed it towards Cayden, it tumbled across the floor and landed a few feet in front of him. Cayden looked down and then back at him.

"What is this?"

"The first part. You get the rest once you hand over

my wife. That's all I want."

One of Cayden's men stepped forward and scooped up the brick. He showed it to Cayden.

"I think you misunderstood our conversation. I told you—"

"I don't give a fuck what you told me. You want this," he said motioning to the bag with a nod. "Then you hand over my wife."

"This is not a negotiation, officer."

"It is if you don't want this to be tossed off the roof."

Cayden stared back, his eyes narrowed. Alex figured he was considering if he was bluffing. "Now I've given you something up front, what do you lose by handing over my wife? You still have a room full of people."

At the far end of the corridor, Alex caught a glimpse of Solomon. There were several apartments between the west stairwell and the homeowners room. It was closer to the west than the east side. Although Cayden's men were distracted by Alex, it was going to take more than that to ensure the safety of the residents.

"How do I know you're not playing games?" Cayden asked.

"Do I look like I would screw around with my wife's life?"

Cayden ran a hand over his head. "Show me the rest."

Alex hesitated for a second but knew he would ask. He dropped down, not taking his eyes off Cayden or his men for even a second. With one hand he unzipped the bag, then lifted one end ever so slightly so Cayden got a good look at the heroin. Satisfied, he rose to his feet.

"Convinced?"

Cayden didn't nod or shrug, he simply smiled as if he was in control.

He pushed Jess forward and she slowly walked towards him. Alex could feel his pulse racing. He saw the look of fear on Jess's face. There was no telling what Cayden would do. It took her less than 60 seconds to walk between them. As soon as he had Jess inside the stairwell he turned back to Cayden.

"It's all yours."

"Throw it over here."

"Sure."

As Alex dropped to a knee, his right arm was out of sight. With one foot holding the stairwell door open, he scooped up his cigarette lighter he'd placed beside the single mason jar with the rag hanging out. He lit the end, and a flame licked over the rag out of view of Cayden and his entourage. Alex scooped up the duffel bag and tossed it a couple of feet ahead of the doorway, then in one smooth motion just as the bag landed and it let out a clinking sound, he tossed the Molotov cocktail straight after. Everything occurred within a matter of seconds. The bag flying through the air, the mason jar following after, the sound of Cayden screaming no, and he and Jess retreating into the safety of the stairwell. Alex didn't see the mason jar land but he heard the explosion.

* * *

Solomon timed it just right. He'd been standing in the west stairwell waiting for Alex to toss the jar before he lit his one and threw it past the homeowners lounge to create a fire on the other side.

Cayden's men were pinned in, surprised and unsure of how to respond. Gunfire erupted as some of them twisted to the sight of flames covering the carpet and creeping up the walls. Solomon darted out and unleashed a flurry of rounds through the flames taking out the two closest to him. The others took cover in the apartments. He darted into the homeowners lounge and began telling everyone to get ready to run for the stairwell.

Standing at the doorway, he wheeled the shotgun around the corner and opened fire while at the same time sending out five at time. A wall of black billowed up creating enough smoke to hide them as they crouched, clung to each other and streamed into the stairwell.

* * *

Alex turned to Jess and told her to head down to the basement.

"I'm not leaving you."

"Solomon needs my help. Jess. Go!" he said waving her off. She hesitated for a second then turned and hurried down as Alex pulled back the door on the fifteenth floor and opened fire from his end, firing only at targets he could make out. By now the entire hallway on the fifteenth floor was a mass of smoke and flames. Tongues of fire licked up the walls, the sound of people coughing and the noise of gunfire dominated.

He pulled back into the stairwell to slap another magazine into the rifle.

They had them pinned in from both sides.

The goal wasn't to kill them as much as it was to give Solomon enough time to get the residents out. If Cayden's men died in the process, so be it. He certainly wasn't firing haphazardly. If there was a clear shot he planned on taking it.

* * *

Cayden pulled back inside the apartment, then unleashed another flurry of rounds at the east stairwell. "Bastard!" he yelled, furious.

"Cayden, the residents are getting out," Vic hollered.

"Kill every one of them," he said before darting out of

the room, and trying to get close to the other stairwell. The flames were intense, he could barely breathe with all the smoke. He called out to Leon. "Leon!"

There was no reply. He looked back and saw most of his men lying on the floor. "Leon!" he screamed and darted over to him, grabbing a hold of the back of his jacket and hauling him into the closest apartment. When he had him inside he flipped him over and looked down at the wound in his stomach.

"Hey, hey, don't you die on me."

He slapped his face a few times and Leon's eyelids opened. Clutching him in his arms he shook his head unable to believe this was happening. Everything was going smoothly. Now his best friend was fighting for his life.

"Leon."

Leon managed to muster a few words. "I told you, Cayden."

Tears welled up in Cayden's eyes. "I know you did."

"Get out now. Look after my kid," he said through

gritted teeth as he winced in death's grip.

"No. No. You're going to do that," Cayden said. "Hang in there, Leon."

Blood trickled out the corner of Leon's mouth and his eyes closed.

"Leon. Leon!" He yelled his name several more times and tried performing CPR on him but it was useless, there was no pulse. Rage overwhelmed him. He no longer cared about the drugs, nor the residents, all he wanted now was to kill that officer. He ran his fingers over his face to close his eyelids.

Cayden staggered to his feet, coughing and spluttering. The smoke was beginning to overwhelm him. He could barely breathe. Outside the apartment he could hear gunfire still erupting. He made his way over to the door and pulled back, then raised his forearm. The flames were intense and had filled almost every inch of the floor.

Resigned to his fate, and fueled by the loss of his friend, he darted out into the corridor, unleashing every round in his magazine at the east stairwell while rushing forward, and jumping through a wall of fire and smoke.

* * *

Rounds ricocheted off the door as Alex pulled back. He was in the middle of slapping another magazine into the rifle when the door burst open and Cayden piled into him. They fell back, over the edge of the top stair, and toppled down twelve steps landing hard.

It was like being attacked by a wild animal. Cayden drove his fist into Alex's face multiple times before Alex managed to wrap his legs around him and twist him off to one side. He squeezed Cayden's neck between his thighs trying to choke him out and for a second he thought he had him as he watched his face turn a beet red, but then Cayden turned his head and bit down.

Alex let out a guttural scream and released him.

Before he had a chance to recover, Cayden began stomping him in the ribs. Pain shot through him as he tried to shield himself from the attack. Three more strikes to the face and everything went black. With the wind knocked out of him, and slipping in and out of consciousness, he felt Cayden latch on to his collar and drag him.

When he came to, he felt himself being hauled up steps and heard Cayden talking to himself. "You've stolen my livelihood. You've stolen everything that's mattered to me. Well now I'm going to steal everything you have starting with your life, then your wife and finally your daughter."

Alex shook his head. The world around him was upside down.

He tried to snap out of the mental fog but as hard as he tried, he kept going unconscious. The next time he awoke, he felt freezing cold wind biting at his ears. The cold snapped his senses back to normal. That's when he realized where he was, in the doorway of the roof.

Cayden was attempting to push him out and let the wind blow him off the roof. And he might have succeeded had it not been for the cold waking him up. Alex used what strength he had in him to latch on to Cayden's leg. He was like a pit bull holding on for dear life.

"Get. Off!" Cayden yelled kicking him again with his free leg.

As painful as it was to hold on, he knew if he released it was over. He wouldn't have the strength to resist the 90 mph winds that had already torn off some of the air vents. Cayden dropped down and tried prying his fingers away but when that didn't work he started punching him in the face, once, twice, three times.

After being knocked so hard in the jaw, his hands released from his leg and he slipped out but just managed to grab hold of a steel pipe near the roof's doorway.

"You bastard just won't die, will you?"

Cayden got on the ground and positioned himself in such a way that half of his body was inside the stairwell and the other half was out. He was trying to use the length of his legs to reach Alex and kick his hands off the steel pipe.

Alex felt the crunch of his boot against his knuckles.

So cold from the wind he could barely feel it.

Cayden inched out a bit further and drew back his leg,

this time hoping to kick him in the face and perhaps it would have worked if what occurred next didn't happen. Something red struck Cayden hard in the head, knocking him out of the doorway and across the roof. Alex turned in time to see him topple like tumbleweed blown by the wind straight over the edge. His scream was lost in the howl of the storm.

Alex squinted, looking back to see who it was, a figure came into view and he smiled. There at the door with a fire extinguisher in her grasp was Jess.

"I told you I wasn't leaving you," she said reaching for his hand.

Chapter 20

Windswept, frozen by the cold and staggering in pain, Alex and Jess made their way down the fourteen-story building. When they reached the second floor there was a long line of people clogging up the stairwell. Agnes spotted Alex and called out to Solomon. A minute or two passed, then he navigated his way up and stopped a few feet in front of them. Alex had his arm slung over Jess and was gripping his ribs with the other hand. A smile flickered on both their faces as he leaned in and squeezed Alex's shoulder.

"One hell of a day, huh?"

"You're telling me," Alex replied.

Solomon motioned with his head. "Well, we are not out of the woods yet. The basement is full now. There's no way to get to the school. However, I've managed to get the lock off the back door and flagged Lucas down. They're taking out people five at a time. It's going to be a long process."

They made their way down the staircase to the first floor. Alex's gaze washed over the crowd of people. "Did everyone make it?" he asked.

"Not everyone," Solomon replied, his chin dropping.

They continued on around to the front of the building and joined the others waiting for a ride. It was a slow process as the weather outside wasn't letting up and only appeared to be getting worse. The waters had risen, seeping into the building and flooding the first floor. Up to their ankles in water they sloshed through the mess and assisted Solomon in getting everyone to safety.

Outside it was dark, and the blizzard had intensified making visibility low. When they finally loaded the last resident into the boat, Alex, Solomon and Jess climbed onboard. The boat bounced over choppy waves that now covered the town. All that could be seen was the silhouette of a few tall buildings above the surface like outstretched fingers. A crescent moon reflected off the water in one area while the rest was covered in snow.

"Where are you taking everyone?" Jess asked.

"A local fisherman, Ted Manning, owns several boats. We'll head out across Prince William Sound and the Passage Canal and head over to Valdez. It's going to be a long journey but hopefully we'll eventually find dry land."

"And if we don't?" Jess asked

Solomon looked back at Alex as they got closer to Ted's boat. "We will."

Alex knew he couldn't guarantee that the rest of the country was in any better shape than Whittier. Whatever had occurred had been drastic enough to cause the waters to rise exponentially. The atmosphere was somber as they were greeted by Ted and climbed onboard. Ted had enough room on his boat for close to thirty people, the rest had to go in two separate boats.

Hayley had been sitting with her knees up and a gray thermal blanket wrapped around her when they spotted her. She squinted, unsure if she was hallucinating. A smile broke on her face and she rushed over, tears filled her eyes as she hugged them tight.

Jess and Alex took a seat beside her and joined the others looking back at the town. No matter what lay ahead Alex had a sense that they would forge forward together. As they pulled away from Whittier, or what was left of it, a lid of heavy white clouds hung over the place, and Begich Towers stood out defiantly as if challenging Mother Nature to bring her worst. It had survived the biggest earthquake in Alaskan history and weathered many storms but this one would truly test its mettle.

Chapter 21

One year later

Tucson, Arizona

Alex sat in a café, soaking in the early morning rays and watching military trucks leave with large numbers of refugees loaded in the back. Families were going home, returning to what was left of the fifty states to rebuild and start again. It would be a struggle but when had life not been hard?

Canada, the USA and many of the northern countries of Europe had suffered greatly during what was called the deadliest storm in recorded history. Over 6.4 million people died across the northern hemisphere and that number appeared to grow with each passing day. There had been wild speculation as to what had caused it, discussions on news channels argued and debated, conspiracy theorists pointed fingers, and climatologists were saying it was the precursor to an even greater event to come if humanity didn't find a solution to global warming. Those who lived in the southern part of the United States had fared well with most heading over into Mexico and seeking asylum in the first few months after the initial hit.

Alex looked over to Jess who was serving coffee to a large line of refugees. In the days and weeks after they'd made it to Anchorage, military helicopters started evacuating people and taking everyone south to where it was warm and dry. Somewhere in the shuffle they had got separated from Solomon and the rest of the Whittier residents, and it had taken close to a month before they saw each other again.

The past twelve months had been tough but a learning experience. The suddenness of the storm had opened even the most skeptical to the dangers of ignoring climate change. The fact was every person's actions had an impact on the environment and if they were to turn back the tide, huge changes would need to be made.

Hayley hurried over and sat down on the bench beside him and tucked her arm around his. "You're up."

"Already? I just sat down," he said.

She pointed at the crowd of people. "Lots of people to serve."

That was one of the prerequisites for staying in the FEMA camp, everyone had to chip in and help, refugees were no different. He was just about to return to serving food and coffee when he spotted Solomon heading over. He ducked under the makeshift green tent that had been set up and assigned as a canteen and café.

"Alex."

"Solomon. Did you find them?"

"Took me a while. Had to ask a lot of questions. They were in a camp west of here." He turned around and motioned to Natalie and his son who were standing near one of the green military trucks.

Alex smiled. "How was she?"

"Natalie is Natalie. We have our issues to work out but I think there's hope."

"Of course there is." He smiled. "I'm pleased for you. So you heading back?"

"Yeah."

"To Whittier?" Alex asked.

"No, actually her family headed to Florida. Jacksonville."

Even after a year many of the cities in the northern hemisphere were unlivable. Whittier, Anchorage and many parts of Canada had got the worst of it.

"What about you?" Solomon asked. "If they ever get it back up and running again, will you return?"

Alex breathed in deeply and looked over to Jess and Hayley. "A wise man once said, if it ever becomes too much, get out. I think I'm going to take his advice."

Solomon grinned, shaking his hand. "I couldn't have said it better myself. It's been good knowing you, kid."

"You too."

Solomon looked over to Natalie who glanced at him. "Well I'll be seeing you."

"I hope not, I think our reunion would be cursed," he

said before both men laughed.

They hugged it out and Alex watched Solomon join his family and climb into the rear of the truck. A soldier banged the side, and it kicked up a plume of dust as it drove away. Hayley called out to Alex, and he twisted around. "Okay, okay, I'm coming."

The storm had tested the resolve of their family and been a wake-up call to humanity. Although many lives were lost, and much was taken from the world they once knew, it had taught them all a valuable lesson, and one that would not be so easily forgotten.

The world they lived in was not a commodity, an inexhaustible resource from which they could draw upon, it had its limits and if they continued to push, it would push back. Climate change was no longer someone else's problem, it was his, his neighbors', and the world at large, and how they dealt with it today would determine the impact of tomorrow.

A Plea

Thank you for reading The Last Storm. If you enjoyed the book, I would really appreciate it if you would consider leaving a review. Without reviews, an author's books are virtually invisible on the retail sites. It also lets me know what you liked. You can leave a review by visiting the book's page. I would greatly appreciate it. It only takes a couple of seconds.

Thank you — **Jack Hunt**

Newsletter

Thank you for buying The Last Storm, published by Direct Response Publishing.

Click here to receive special offers, bonus content, and news about new Jack Hunt's books. Sign up for the newsletter. http://www.jackhuntbooks.com/signup/

About the Author

Jack Hunt is the author of horror, sci-fi and post-apocalyptic novels. He currently has three books out in the War Buds Series, Four Books out in the EMP Survival series, Two books in the Wild Ones series, three in the Camp Zero series, five books out in the Renegades series, three books in the Agora Virus series, one called Blackout, one called Final Impact, one called Darkest Hour, one out in the Armada series, a time travel book called Killing Time and another called Mavericks: Hunters Moon. Jack lives on the East coast of North America.

www.ingramcontent.com/pod-product-compliance
Lightning Source LLC
LaVergne TN
LVHW040241110625
813592LV00021B/126

* 9 7 8 1 7 2 1 7 6 8 8 3 7 *